WRITERS AND THEIR WORK

VICTORIAN QUEST ROMANCE

'My God - Roget's Thesaurus!'

Ronald Searle (1920 -) treats Conan Doyle's *The Lost World* to a cross-linguistic pun. (In Greek the noun 'thesauros' denotes treasure; the suffix '-sauros' means a lizard.) From *Souls in Torment* (London: Perpetua, 1953).

VICTORIAN QUEST ROMANCE

Stevenson, Haggard, Kipling, and Conan Doyle

Robert Fraser

NORTHCOTE

BRITISH COUNCIL

ATLANTIC
PUBLISHERS & DISTRIBUTORS (P) LTD

This edition is published by

ATLANTIC

PUBLISHERS & DISTRIBUTORS (P) LTD

7/22, Ansari Road, Darya Ganj, New Delhi-110 002
Tel: 40775252, 23273880, 23275880, 23280451; Fax: +91-11-23285873
E-mail: orders@atlanticbooks.com; Web: www.atlanticbooks.com

By arrangement with
Northcote House Publishers Ltd
Horndon House, Horndon, Tavistock, Devon, PL19 9NQ,
United Kingdom. (T)+44(0)1822 810066; (F)+44(0)1822 810034
(E) northcote.house@virgin.net and (W) www.northcotehouse.co.uk
The *Writers and their Work* series is published in association with the British Council.

First Indian Reprint 2010
First published in 1998 by Northcote House Publishers Ltd

ISBN 978-81-269-1317-6

British Library Cataloguing-in-Publication Data
A catalogue record for this book is available from the British Library

Typeset by PDQ Typesetting, Newcastle-under-Lyme
Printed in India at Nice Printing Press, A-33/3A, Site-IV,
Industrial Area, Sahibabad, Ghaziabad, U.P.

For Ben Okri

Contents

Preface

To do full justice to travel and adventure fiction in the nineteenth century would require a tome of many hundreds of pages. Within the limited physical scope provided by this series, all that an author can hope for is to plot a course. What follows is not a survey, but an interpretative essay in which I have attempted to outline a few approaches to the Victorian quest writing, and to test my ideas against a select group of texts, well known for the most part, by writers who are still widely read.

I have tried to situate such writing in the context of the marked acceleration in the human and physical sciences that characterized the late nineteenth century. To what extent, I ask, are the more interesting quest romances of the time responses to these developments? Adventure literature is sometimes construed as a means of escape, or of indulgence in compensatory fantasy. Certain recent accounts have portrayed it as acting, in the period in question, as a tacit expression of power. These chapters are concerned with the alternative possibility that for the late Victorians such stories were modes of understanding, even of knowledge.

Manifestly, such an angle is relevant to writers, and to cultural forms, other than those chosen. For the inquisitive, some indication of the broader scene may be found in the Chronology. In the main text, it seemed wisest to restrict discussion to texts that commonly engage us. This book is not a map, but a compass.

Robert Fraser

Acknowledgements

Warm thanks are due to the Centre for English Studies in the University of London, and to Professor Warwick Gould its Programme Director, for an Honorary Research Fellowship during the completion of this short study. I would like to record my appreciation to Professor Isobel Armstrong, General Editor of *Writers and their Work,* for commissioning the title in the first instance, and for enhancing my appreciation of the Victorian period through her conversation and published work. I am indebted to John Hamill and the library staff at Freemasons Hall for information about the Craft, to John Villiers, stalwart scholar of the East, for details of the founding of the Royal Asiatic and Hakluyt societies, and to Ruth Fletcher for acting as cicerone at Bateman's, Kipling's home in Sussex. On that and other adventures I have learned much about the spirit of the quest from my son, Benjo; my wife, Catherine, has been a lively accomplice in romance.

Chronology

1815 The Treaty of Vienna brings the Napoleonic Wars to a close.

1822 Dr Gideon Mantell describes a prehistoric lizard called the iguanodon in his book *The Fossils of the South Downs*.

1826 Foundation of the Royal Asiatic Society 'for the investigation of subjects connected with, and for the encouragement of science, literature and the arts in relation to Asia', under its first director Henry Thomas Colebrooke, Sanskrit scholar, previously of the East India Company and the Asiatic Society of Bengal.

1830 The pterodactyl, an extinct winged reptile, is alluded to in Charles Lyell's *Principles of Geology*. A meeting of 'members of the Raleigh Travellers' Club and several other gentlemen' on 24 May sets up the Royal Geographical Society to disseminate 'just and distinct notions of the physical and political relations of our globe'.

1837 Thomas Carlyle's *The French Revolution*; accession of Queen Victoria.

1838 First stretch of the Great Western Railway opens on 4 June.

1841 Thomas Carlyle's *On Heroes, Hero-Worship and the Heroic in History*. Thomas Cook, Secretary of the Leicester Temperance Society, launches his first excursion on 5 July.

1843 Tennyson's *The Morte d'Arthur*.

1846 Founding of the Hakluyt Society to 'edit and print for distribution among the members records of the Voyages, Travels, Naval Expeditions, and other geographical material, and to promote the knowledge of these matters', named after Richard Hakluyt (1552?–1616), English antiquarian, archdeacon of Westminster, and sometime ambassador in Paris.

1850 Robert Louis Stevenson born in Edinburgh.

1851 The Great Exhibition of the Industry of All Nations opens in Paxton's Crystal Palace, featuring an 'Indian Court' and displays devoted to Africa, the West Indies, and the Cape of Good Hope, as well as a section on Egypt.

1855 Charles Kingsley's *The Heroes*.

1856 Henry Rider Haggard born in Bradenham, Norfolk.

1857 Tom Hughes's *Tom Brown's Schooldays*. South Kensington Museum opens its doors. Mutiny by Indian sepoys provokes the Crown into wresting control of the subcontinent from the East India Company. Burton and Speke search East Africa for the head of the White Nile; after Burton succumbs to malaria, Speke believes himself to have found the source at Lake Victoria.

1859 Darwin's *On the Origin of Species*. Arthur Conan Doyle born in Edinburgh.

1861 Jacob Bachofen's *Das Mutterrecht*. Death of Albert, Prince Consort.

1862 International Exhibition in South Kensington.

1863 Jules Verne's *Cinq semaines en ballon; voyage et découvertes en Afrique par trois anglais [Five Weeks in a Balloon: Travels and Discoveries in Africa by Three Englishmen]*.

1865 J. F. M'Lennan's *Primitive Marriage*; Jules Verne's *De la Terre à la Lune [From the Earth to the Moon]*. Rudyard Kipling born in Bombay. Diamonds discovered in South Africa.

1869 Henry Sumner Maine's *Ancient Law*. Jules Verne's *Vingt mille lieues sous les mers [Twenty Thousand Leagues under the Sea]*.

1871 Edward Burnett Tylor's *Primitive Culture*; Darwin's *The Descent of Man*. Foundation of the Royal Anthropological Institute. Stanley meets Livingston at Ujiji on Lake Tanganyika.

1873 Thomas Cook's first round-the-world tour. Jules Verne's *Le Tour du monde en quatre-vingts jours [Around the World in Eighty Days]*. Haggard attends Spiritualist seances in London. He is appointed personal assistant to Sir Henry Bulwer, Lieutenant-Governor elect of Natal, accompanying him to South Africa the following year.

1876 Disraeli's government bestows on Victoria the title 'Empress of India'.

1877 Helen Petrovna Blavatsky's *Isis Unveiled: A Master-Key to the Mysteries of Ancient and Modern Science and Technology*. The British annex the Boer Transvaal. On May 24 – Victoria's birthday – Haggard hoists the Union Jack in Pretoria; in August he is appointed Master and Registrar of the High Court at the age of 21.

1879 The Zulus rise under Cetywayo; British troops obliterated at Isandhlwana (22 January); Garnet Wolseley dispatched from London to organize hasty settlement.

1881 Opening of Natural History Museum. First Boer War, at the conclusion of which treaty reinstating self-government for the Transvaal under British suzerainty is drafted in Haggard's farmhouse in Natal.

1882 Haggard's *Cetywayo and his White Neighbours*. Gladstone's government rescues the Khedive of Egypt from insurrection, later occupying Egypt to protect the Suez Canal.

1883 Stevenson's *Treasure Island* appears in book form. Disguised as a hakim or native doctor, William Walter McNair enters Kafiristan.

1884 Andrew Lang's *Custom and Myth*. King Leopold of the Belgians, son of Victoria's Uncle Leopold, convenes Berlin conference on the partition of Africa.

1885 Spurred by the success of *Treasure Island*, and a bet from his brother, Haggard writes *King Solomon's Mines* in six weeks. The manuscript is forwarded by W. E. Henley to Andrew Lang; he writes to Haggard 'I almost prefer it to *Treasure Island*.' Lang persuades Cassells to publish the book; he nominates Haggard for the Savile Club. The Amir of Afghanistan attends Durbah at Rawlpindi, which Kipling reports for *The Civil and Military Gazette*; in September Kipling is received as a Freemason in Lahore. Last stand and death of General Gordon in Khartoum, later mocked memorably in Lytton Strachey's *Eminent Victorians* (1918).

1887 Publication of Haggard's *She* followed by *Allan Quatermain*, which, however, had been written first; J. G. Frazer's *Totemism*. Golden Jubilee of Victoria's accession. First Colonial Conference. Cecil Rhodes forms the British South African Company to exploit regions to the north of the Transvaal.

1888 'The Man Who Would Be King' appears in India as part of *The Phantom Rickshaw and Other Stories*.

1889 Kipling returns to London; he is nominated for the Savile by Lang and Haggard. British infiltration of Matabeleland.

1890 First edition of J. G. Frazer's *The Golden Bough*. British infiltration of Mashonaland.

1894 Kipling's first *Jungle Book*. Mary Kingsley's first West African expedition. Stevenson dies of a haemorrhage in Vailima, Samoa.

1895 Kipling's second *Jungle Book*. H. G. Wells's *The Time Machine*. Mary Kingsley's second West African expedition.

1897 Mary Kingsley's *Travels in West Africa*; Kipling's *Captains Courageous*.

1899 Outbreak of Second Boer War, which Kipling follows keenly.

1900 H. G. Wells's *The First Men on the Moon*; second edition of *The Golden Bough* implicitly debunks Christianity. Ladysmith and Mafeking relieved. Whilst serving as a nurse, Mary Kingsley dies of enteric fever in Simonstown.

1901 Kipling's *Kim*. Death of Queen Victoria. Stegosaurus first classified as distinct genus of dinosaur. The African Society (later the Royal African Society) is founded to perpetuate Mary Kingsley's memory, and with the object of studying the 'languages, institutions, customs, religions and antiquities of Africa.'

1902 Second Boer War ends at the Peace of Vereeniging.

1903 Lang's *The Book of Romance*.

1912 Conan Doyle's *The Lost World*.

1914 Outbreak of the First World War.

Abbreviations

AQ H. Rider Haggard, *Allan Quatermain, being an account of his further adventures and discoveries in company with Sir Henry Curtis, Bart, Commander John Good R.N. and one Umslopogaas*, ed. Dennis Butts (World's Classics; Oxford: Oxford University Press, 1995)

C. H. Rider Haggard, *Cetywayo and his White Neighbours, or Remarks on Recent Events in Zululand, Natal and Transvaal* (London: Trübner, 1882)

DML H. Rider Haggard, *The Days of My Life*, ed. C. J. Longman (2 vols.; London: Longman, 1926)

JB Rudyard Kipling, *The Jungle Books*, ed. W. W. Robson (World's Classics; Oxford: Oxford University Press, 1992)

K. Rudyard Kipling, *Kim*, ed. Alan Sandison (World's Classics; Oxford: Oxford University Press, 1987)

KSM H. Rider Haggard, *King Solomon's Mines*, ed. Dennis Butts (World's Classics; Oxford: Oxford University Press, 1989)

LW Arthur Conan Doyle, *The Lost World: Being an Account of the Recent Amazing Adventures of Professor George E. Challenger, Lord Roxton, Professor Summerlee and Mr. E. D. Malone of 'The Daily Gazette'* (Oxford Popular Fiction; Oxford: Oxford University Press, 1995)

MA Arthur Conan Doyle, *Memories and Adventures* (London: Hodder & Stoughton, 1924)

MK Rudyard Kipling, *The Man Who Would Be King and Other Stories*, ed. Louis Cornell (World's Classics; Oxford: Oxford University Press, 1987)

RKRH *Rudyard Kipling to Rider Haggard: The Record of a Friendship*, ed. Morton Cohen (London: Hutchinson, 1965)

S. H. Rider Haggard, *She: A History of Adventure*, ed. Daniel Karlin (World's Classics; Oxford: Oxford University

Press, 1991)

SOM Rudyard Kipling, *Something of Myself: For My Friends, Known and Unknown* (London: Macmillan, 1937)

TI Robert Louis Stevenson, *Treasure Island*, ed. Emma Letley (World's Classics; Oxford: Oxford University Press, 1985)

WWS Arthur Conan Doyle, *When the World Screamed*, in *The Lost World and Other Stories* (Wordsworth Classics; Ware: Wordsworth Editions, 1995)

1

The Quest

The subject of this little book is a particular fictional genre, and four writers who practised it. The genre is quest narrative, sometimes known as 'quest romance', and the authors – all male, and three of them personal friends – were Robert Louis Stevenson, Henry Rider Haggard, Rudyard Kipling, and Arthur Conan Doyle. Strongly contrasted personalities, all four were travelled people who, in a characteristically Victorian way, combined marked practical aptitude with a countervailing tendency towards mysticism. Valuing self-discipline, all none the less experienced occasional fits of restlessness, even of inner blackness or turmoil. All were memorably exposed to cultures outside Europe, where they picked up local knowledge that coloured their fiction. Products of the mid-Victorian age, they inherited the cultural assurance of their time. Yet in each of them these standard convictions coexisted with an inveterate curiosity about, and respect for, other cultures, which seems at odds with their acquiescence in the status quo.

Other, sometimes paradoxical, qualities connect these writers. Each was an uxorious and devoted husband who cherished the company of his male friends. Introspective, they were also intensely clubbable. Indeed, three of them belonged to exactly the same London club: the Savile, then situated in Piccadilly. It was on the premises of the Savile that Haggard and Kipling first met, introduced to one another by the Scottish folklorist Andrew Lang, himself a writer and theorist of quest romance, who had proposed each of them for membership. It was as fellow members of the Savile that both received felicitations on his early work from Stevenson, a corresponding member resident in Samoa. Though Stevenson was to die before meeting either man in the flesh, the feeling of kinship did not die with him. The bond between these writers was as much personal as it was literary, reinforcing a shared sensation of regarding the world through much the same eyes.

Arguably, the genre which these authors perfected was the vehicle for this common vision. Quest narrative was the product of a number of factors that came together in the late 1880s. Though its roots lie deep, stretching as far back as classical literature, the cultural mix of high imperialism – a more complex phenomenon than is sometimes realized – brought these strands together to form a unique variety of tale which has had its imitators even in our own day, but which existed in its pure form only for about forty years: between say 1880 and 1920. The reasons for this are diverse, and have much to do with the way in which the male Victorian mind adjusted both to the pressures of colonial experience, and to various stresses within British society itself.

Recently, quest romance has attracted renewed attention from critics. The reasons for this revitalized interest tell us as much about our own predispositions as they do about the form itself. We live in a postcolonial age, one of the privileges of which is that we assess the work of the Victorians with apparent detachment. After all, so we tend to argue, we no longer share their prejudices, and are free from the need to justify a – to us – repugnant style of mastery. Stevenson, Haggard, Kipling, and Conan Doyle strike us as artists of modest talent, trapped and limited by time. It is the illusion of every period that its point of view is more objective than that of previous ages. Since the fetters of imperialism have fallen away, along with the blinkers that its supporters wore, we flatter ourselves that we can now see its cultural products for what they really were. Having freed the Empire, postcolonialism has, we now believe, liberated us.

Apparently, this emancipation has empowered the critics. Unencumbered by the pressures of the past, they have permitted their sensibilities to float freely, picking up, through postmodern or postfeminist association, meanings and affinities in late-Victorian travel romance to which its writers and first readers were, they believe, blind. For instance, the fact that these authors were men writing for a predominantly male audience has not escaped attention. In her study of late-Victorian sexual and literary mores, *Sexual Anarchy,* Elaine Showalter has interpreted this phenomenon as one aspect of a shift apparent in the 1880s away from the three-volume novel popular in the middle decades of Queen Victoria's reign. The 'triple decker' had often been written by women – George Eliot was its supreme exponent – and women made up the larger share of its readership. By 1880, she argues, men had grown tired of this female hegemony. Appropriately, they withdrew into their London clubs, where they developed a style of shorter fiction, from the plots of which the ladies were resolutely banished. 'The revival of romance in the 1880's', Showalter concludes, 'was a men's literary revolution intended to reclaim the kingdom of the English novel for male writers, male readers, and men's stories.'[1] On this view such adventures were deliberately set in remote parts of the globe in which European women were not welcome, and featured feats of endurance calculated to boost masculine self-esteem. Moreover, Showalter argues, the camaraderie evident in these narratives bolstered a male myth of self-nurturing intended to keep women at a distance, and to confine creativity to a homosocial, potentially to a homoerotic, zone.

Other accounts of Victorian quest narrative have concentrated on the political relations implicit within it. For Edward Said, such writing is a strategy to enhance the might of empire by denying the validity of subordinate cultures. In Said's eyes, these works are rife with a peculiar kind of curiosity: the fascination felt by a beast of prey for its victim. In such books, he declares in *Culture and Imperialism*, 'we discern a new narrative progression and triumphalism. Almost without exception these narratives, and literally hundreds of them based on the exhilaration and interest of adventure in the colonial world, far from casting doubt on the imperial undertaking, serve to confirm and celebrate its success.'[2]

Perceptive to a degree though Showalter's and Said's remarks are, we need to be aware of the barely concealed note of postcolonial hubris present in them. Current modes of reading may indeed enable us to see Victorian travel romance in a stark, oblique light, disclosing insights which its proponents would have resisted, even if they had understood them. Doubtless, too, historical hindsight permits us to dismantle the ideas supporting the vogue for adventure romance or, as we say, to 'deconstruct' it. The question is whether the edifices which we then assemble out of the pieces possess any more solidity than those we have taken down.

To put the issue another way, we have grown used to checking the literature of a century ago against ideologies which lie midway in time between us and its creation. The psychological theories of Freud and Lacan are a common source of such readings. The feminist programmes of Hélène Cixous or of Showalter represent another potent influence. The post-colonial perspectives of Frantz Fanon, Said, Gyatri Spivak, or Homi Bhaba offer a third. The question is whether such techniques of interpretation disclose deep structures within the work, or whether they simply encourage us to acclimatize late Victorian literature to our own cultural ecology.

The Victorians were as interested in the relationship between inspiration, culture, and environment as we are. By examining their environment closely – especially, though not exclusively, its material conditions – we may be able to discern patterns as invisible to the writers of travel romance themselves as they are to critics of our own day, driven by its successive '-isms'.

2

'The catawampus of Romance'

Catawampus: a. & n. & slang. (chiefly N. Amer) As adj. also -ous. [origin unknown] A. adj. Fierce, destructive; askew, awry. B. n. A fierce imaginary animal.

Shorter Oxford Dictionary

THE PREHISTORY OF ROMANCE

As the Victorians were well aware, tales describing groups of men departing for unknown destinations in search of wealth, or to quell some peril, are as old as the art of storytelling itself. In *Myth, Ritual and Religion,* his treatise of 1887 on the relation between legend and belief, Andrew Lang lists several such legends which are so widely diffused over the world that their point of origin is impossible to locate.[1] Among the most common that he mentions is the story known to the Greeks as 'Jason and the Argonauts'. Yet Jason is only one of a whole series of male protagonists who, in stories found in various parts of the world, set out with a team of picked companions to recover a golden fleece, or the skin of some fabulous animal. Tales such as this are to be found in Homer, Mimnermus, Apollonius Rhodius, and Euripides, but the motif is also recognizable in folk tales from non-European cultures. For the Victorians, who had noted these coincidences, the question therefore arose: had the folk tales borrowed from literary epic, or epic from the folk tales?

Though the subject of priority proved difficult to resolve, one fact was clear: romances such as 'Jason and the Argonauts' formed one element in a trio, the other items in which were myths, and the stories told to children. As early as 1810, in the

Preface to *The Lady of the Lake*, Sir Walter Scott had spelled out this equation: 'The mythology of one period,' he had written, 'would seem to pass into the romance of the next, and that into the nursery tales of subsequent ages.' In other words, so late Victorians came to believe, people had begun with certain beliefs, which they had then embodied as legends. These were in turn handed down from generation to generation until they 'degenerated' – a word often used by late-Victorian folklorists – into fairy stories. The relationship between such stories and romance was of paramount importance to nineteenth-century theories of fiction, and determined contemporary thinking about the certain kinds of narrative. For Scott, for Lang, and for most of the writers considered in this study, to read a romance was, therefore, in some sense pleasurably to regress.

Whatever theory was used to explain the universality of such stories, it is clear that certain key features of travel romance are already present in the traditional legends: news of distant danger, a foregathering of male companions determined to pursue it, an onerous journey across uncharted regions, the reaching of the goal, the conquest, a withdrawal. The story of Jason even features a female figure – Medea – who alternately assists in the quest, and disturbs the process of the event.

The term 'romance' itself is medieval, and is all the more confusing because it is etymologically related to *roman*, the French word for a 'novel'. This coincidence is no matter for surprise, since, beginning in the sixteenth century, the novel itself slowly evolved out of the medieval romance – or rather out of Cervantes's merciless pillorying of medieval motifs in *Don Quixote*, which itself describes a journey. With Cervantes, however, a gulf opens up between narratives purporting to recount the everyday, and stories revelling in the marvellous – a divergence which has important consequences for the development of European fiction.

Of all the medieval romances, none was more attractive to the Victorian age than the cluster of stories surrounding King Arthur. In 1842, when Tennyson published 'The Morte d'Arthur', subsequently incorporated into his *Idylls of the King* (1859–85), he was cashing in on a vogue, but he also sustained and strengthened it. Tennyson's sources were Chrétien de Troyes and Malory – above all the second. In whatever form they were first encountered, however, the Arthurian stories rapidly became a staple of Victorian childhood reading. Indeed, by the last quarter of the century, enthusiasm for Arthur and the Knights of the Round Table amounted almost to a craze. Rider Haggard, for example, called his son Arthur, and Arthur was Conan Doyle's Christian name. In 1903 Lang gathered these legends together in his *The Book of Romance*, shaping them so as to highlight elements which were important to writers of contemporary quest romance: the band of companions devoted to one another; the common code of chivalry; the quest for a fabled source of wisdom; forbearance; virility; fighting. In Guinevere he portrayed a figure in which many of the ambivalent feelings towards women of the Victorian age were concentrated, feelings common to Victorian males and absorbed in childhood: the dream of a figure at once remote and pure, passionate and complicated, a solace and occasionally a danger, a common ideal who was at the same time a cause for dissension.

The literary ancestry of late-nineteenth-century travel romance is thus comparatively clear, all the more so because writers of the time tended to stress it. All of the exponents of what we have come to know as Victorian 'male quest narrative' were immersed in the accepted common sources. In his autobiography *The Days of My Life*, Haggard talks of his childhood reading in the nursery, the staple of which was the Arthurian tales and versions of classical romance. In *Something of Myself*, Kipling recalls going to stay with his Aunt Georgie, wife of the painter Edward Burne-Jones, at The Grange, North End Road, where she would read him '*The Pirate* or *The Arabian Nights* of evenings, when one lay on the big sofas sucking toffee' (*SOM* 12). Interestingly, both men also seem to have believed that the Arabian Nights and the Arthurian cycle, like other classical or medieval romances, were not 'literary' in the narrow sense. So integral were such stories to their culture, so close did people's first acquaintance with them lie to infancy, that romance seems to have approximated in the eyes of late-Victorian people to what we now call 'orature', something handed down by word of mouth.

Perhaps for this reason, the tone of voice in the literary romances of the late-Victorian age is very often that of a father speaking to his sons, or maybe of an elder brother mesmerizing his juniors: a voice familiar, coaxing, teasing, admonitory by turns. Another reason is that myths and romantic stories frequently convey and consolidate the common values of a culture. In this they contrast with the novel, the purport of which is often to be critical of its times. The values of Greek tales are those of Hellenic civilization; the values of medieval romances are those of Christian chivalry. In this respect the fabulators of the Victorian age were no different from those that they emulated. As well as providing enjoyment, romances should, they believed, instruct. A clear exposition of this view can be found in Charles Kingsley's *The Heroes*, his reworking of several Greek quest legends – including those of Jason, Perseus, and Theseus – written in 1855, and dedicated to 'My Children Rose, Maurice and Mary'. In its preface he calls attention to the universality of quest romance, and explains why, in his view, the Greeks had cultivated such writing:

> All nations do so when they are young: our old forefathers did, and called their stories 'Sagas'. I will read you some of them some day – some of the Eddas, and the Voluspa, and Beowulf, and the noble old Romances. The old Arabs, again had their tales, which we now call the 'Arabian Nights'. The old Romans had theirs, and they called them 'Fabulae', from which our word 'fable' comes; but the old Hellenes called theirs 'Muthoi' from which our new word 'myth' is taken. But next to those old Romances, which were written in the Christian middle age, there are no fairy tales like these old Greek ones, for beauty, and wisdom, and truth, and making children love noble deeds, and trust in God to help them through.[2]

The effortless transition from cultural history to sermonizing in this passage – and its appropriation of pagan for avowedly Christian ends – are typical of Kingsley, but in a subtler form such thinking slips into the tone of much late Victorian romance writing. Courage and steadfastness were cardinal virtues around which, in the heyday of the mid-Victorian Broad Church, Christian virtue quite naturally arranged itself. The essence of integrity was that it should be put, morally and physically, to the test. Since adventure romance depicted valour, it was the ideal vehicle for stressing the importance of certain kinds of endurance. And of all ways of testing such fortitude, the most attractive was a journey.

From where had the Victorians derived this highly distinctive conception of virtue? The simplest answer is they owed it to Thomas Carlyle, who in his lecture course of 1841 *On Heroes, Hero-Worship, and the Heroic in History* had expounded a highly personal dialectic, depicting the interplay between the human personality and the turmoil of circumstantial events.[3] History – the French Revolution, for example, a subject about which, in the year of Victoria's accession, Carlyle had published his greatest work – was a forge on which the weapons of the human soul were beaten out. Danger, in Carlyle's eyes, was productive – a view from which few Victorian males dissented, at least until Oscar Wilde.

The surprising facet of Carlyle's teaching to later readers is the extent to which he portrayed virtue as male. 'Manly' is an epithet which slid effortlessly into many mid-Victorian catalogues of goodness, with effects that seem to us insidious. In *Tom Brown's Schooldays*, Tom Hughes ventriloquizes a homily delivered by Dr Samuel Arnold, the inspirational headmaster, to the boys of Rugby school, sometime in the 1840s. It runs: 'Quit yourselves like men, then; speak up, and strike out if necessary for whatsoever is true, and manly, and lovely, and of good report.'[4] Apart from 'manly', all the adjectives in this list come from a passage in which St Paul is exhorting the early Christians in his Epistle to the Philippians (Phil. 4: 8). Hughes's inclusion of manliness distorts the list, but it also aligns virility with a lot of other qualities with which we would not necessarily associate it: sensitivity, responsiveness, even imagination. Indeed, in the face of all the facts, the idea of 'imagination' as a distinctively male trait survived until late in the nineteenth century. When both were old men, Haggard received a compliment from his friend Kipling: 'He thinks that imagination such as mine is the sign or expression of unusual virility, a queer theory that may have something in it' (*RKRH* 107).

For many present-day readers, the most alien element in the code of honour supporting Victorian romance is the perception of fighting as a trial of merit. To us this seems quaint, even perverted, since the political history of the twentieth century had taught us to view 'violence' as repugnant as an end, and questionable even as a means. However, the portrayal of physical conflict in Victorian romance has to be seen partly against the insistence on valour in earlier Romances, and partly against prevailing conceptions of moral courage. Again, one can do no better than quote the author of *Tom Brown's Schooldays*, a book which all the late-Victorian writers of travel romance had almost certainly read:

> Every one who is worth his salt has enemies, who must be beaten, be they evil thoughts and habits in himself, or spiritual wickedness in high places, or Russians, or Border-ruffians, or Bill, Tom, Harry, who will not let him live his life in quiet until he has thrashed them.
>
> It is no good for Quakers, or any other body of men to uplift their voices against fighting. Human nature is too strong for them, and they don't follow their own precepts. Every soul of them is doing his own piece of fighting, one way or another. The world might be a better world without fighting, for anything I know, but it wouldn't be our world; and therefore I am dead against crying peace when there is no peace, and isn't meant to be. I am as sorry as any man to see folk fighting the wrong people and wrong things, but I'd sooner see them doing that, than that they should have no fight in them.[5]

In the terms set out by Hughes, we have all turned nowadays into pacifists or 'Quakers', but many Victorian males thought otherwise. Fighting the good fight with all their might, they convinced themselves that virtue was a variety of soldiery, and soldiery a sign of virtue. The equation in later Victorian romance is seldom as crude as it is in *Tom Brown's Schooldays*, but the ideology of what is sometimes known as 'Muscular Christianity' infiltrates it at every point.

Pervasive as these values had been in mid-Victorian society, unsurprisingly the great women novelists of the period had tended to regard them askance. Forbearance and courage are certainly themes in George Eliot and Mrs Gaskell, but they are subordinate to other overwhelming concerns: social justice, for example, and transformation of the countryside through industrialization. At the end of Gaskell's *North and South*, published in 1854, Margaret Hale, who is about at long last to accept the masterful but impulsive factory owner John Thornton in marriage, counsels him on the need for patience and restraint. Characteristically, the advice is delivered by a woman to a man, and its significance is only part of the novelist's meaning. In the last quarter of the century, something seems to have happened to alter this priority: to bring out and make available a more overt male element in fiction, and to turn the pursuit of adventure into a prime topic for some male writers. The reasons for this development are complicated, and involve a cultural shift which took place towards the *fin-de-siècle*. There were many symptoms of this change: the rise of exclusive male clubs; changes in dress which eventually led men to clothe themselves in sober grey or black; the outlawing of homosexuality in 1885, to name but three. The rise of male quest romance, however, is best viewed against a transformation in literary sensibility in the late 1880s and early 1890s brought about by developments in publishing.

THE REVIVAL OF QUEST ROMANCE

Shifts in literary fashion are often symptomatic of deeper shifts in society; they are also often shaped by something as superficially unglamorous as the economics of book production. The prevailing forms of fiction in the mid-Victorian period had been heavily influenced by the needs of periodicals and circulating libraries, to whom publishers customarily gave large discounts. The most popular format was the three-volume novel, the publication of which was timed to coincide with the last, or last-but-one, episode of the story in a magazine. Large-scale novels were the norm, catering for a need for leisurely reading, and ensuring a satisfyingly deferred conclusion to the tale. In 1894, however, the trade agreement between publishers and circulating libraries which upheld this system collapsed, because the publishers withdrew the subsidy. Since the advantages of deferred publication no longer pertained, shorter, one-volume novels with snappy, incisive plots became newly attractive. One result of this change was a boost for the short story; another was a burgeoning of one-volume romances.[6]

Already, however, a shift in taste was under way. In October 1889, when Kipling arrived back from India and was promptly nominated by Lang for membership of the Savile Club, he found its habitués torn between advocates of 'the crocodile of Realism and the catawampus of Romance' (*RKRH* 15). The catawampus is a fictitious animal of the American swamps, whose teeth are supposed to be strong enough to devour other amphibians. Already, it seemed to Kipling, romance was in danger of devouring the 'realistic' novel whole. Of course, this process was very far from a complete one; Kipling's sense of their incompatibility, however, raises the question of how the late Victorians viewed the difference between these two genres.

I have already mentioned the historical connection between romances and myths. Probably the most common way in which the Victorians thought about quest romance was as a narrative prose form which retained the shape and trajectory of epic or myth, while keeping in touch with the modern world through its physical context, its characterization, and its dialogue. The novel, by contrast, was seen as concentrating on verisimilitude, departures from which were felt to be contrived, even to amount to artistic flaws. At no point in the history of either genre, it has to be stressed, was this distinction seen as absolute. We speak of elements of romance in the novel: in this sense we can describe Dickens, with his leanings towards caricature and the fabulous, as a more 'romantic' novelist than say Trollope. Equivalently, we also refer to 'novelistic' ingredients in romance. Be that as it may, by the late 1880s, when this study begins, the two forms were commonly regarded, not simply as distinct, but as rival kinds of fiction.

The cultural causes of this development are often simplified. Exponents of the New Historicist school of criticism such as Showalter have argued that the new popularity of travel romance had much to do with a cultural reaction by male writers against what they perceived as a female hegemony in fiction. By 1889, on this view, male writers came to feel that the dominance of women novelists over the previous few decades had represented an imbalance of gender.[7] In the eyes of certain more bigoted critics, this supremacy had gone along with a suppression of the fanciful and adventurous in favour of the ordinary and everyday. In 1887, for example, when Haggard's *She* was an overnight success, the novelist and popular historian Sir Walter Besant wrote to its author, telling him not to be discouraged by sour reactions from female reviewers: 'If the critic is a woman she will put down this book with the remark that it is impossible – almost all women have this feeling towards the marvellous.'[8]

The overt sexual chauvinism of Besant's remark should not blind us to one aspect of its logic which has important implications for the way that Besant's contemporaries viewed the rise of the quest. Besant's female critic is envisaged as dismissing *She* on the grounds of its implausibility. The fact that Besant portrays this anticipated reaction as unjust suggests that in his eyes, and implicitly in Haggard's, the marvellous and exceptional were not only feasible, but potentially as true as the everyday. We may add that a convincing adventure romance explores this paradox, and persuades us of its cogency. The strength of the romance, by this token, has to do with its treatment of the ambiguous, versatile relationship between believability and fact.

Of course, a sense of what is, or is not, believable has very little to do with gender. None the less, even at a distance of more than a century, it is possible to see what Besant and his contemporaries felt they were reacting against. The finest novels by mid-Victorian women had been feats of perceptive social observation. They had, however, been markedly less enthusiastic about a different sort of truth – that pertaining to arcane and esoteric knowledge. Eliot and Gaskell were deeply interested in the typical and the general; they gave shorter shrift to varieties of knowledge which made no obvious contribution to the welfare of society. *Middlemarch*, for example, features two narrow specialists, both male, whose preoccupation with recondite knowledge, though admirable, is viewed as ultimately detrimental to their full human responsiveness. The mythographer Casaubon is so steeped in abstruse researches into the mythology of the ancient Orient that he fails to make an adequate husband for Dorothea Brooke. After his death, she makes a more satisfactory union with the dilettante Will Ladislaw, who himself regards her first husband's scholarly obsessions as amounting to a set of 'mouldy futilities'. Dr Tertius Lydgate spends much of the novel searching for a primitive organic tissue underlying all other physiological manifestations. His search for this medical Holy Grail is as doomed to failure as are Casaubon's delvings into the learned dust of myth: he entirely fails to satisfy his wife Rosamund Vincy, and drifts catastrophically into debt.

The implied judgement on the failure of these two characters is all the more instructive since Eliot was more interested in, and informed about, mythology and science than most of her male contemporaries. The fact remains that her scientific affinities, for example, are submerged in the deep structure of her work, where, as Gillian Beer has established, they operate on the level of analogies for her own fictional procedures.[9] By contrast, Casaubon's and Lydgate's professional obsession with abstruse knowledge, their mania for out-of-the-way information, their eagerness to impress a diffuse male peer group of experts, are diminished by Eliot's shrewd female scepticism, which sees them as limiting to individual and collective wholeness.

In 1887, Lang wrote that fiction was like a shield. The novel represented its 'silver side', reflecting 'the study of manners and of character'; romance was its 'golden side', revealing the extraordinary and out of the way.[10] Lang's enthusiasm for this 'golden side' had much to do with his sense that the extraordinary was as likely to be true as the ordinary. For the advocates of romance, the esoteric and outlandish were newly worthy of attention, not simply because they permitted an escape from commonplace tedium, but because they opened onto the wilder excesses of fact.

In the closing years of the nineteenth century, this perception received an effective boost from two related developments. The first was the rapid expansion of the Empire, dispatching administrators, engineers, and missionaries to far-flung places, from which they sent back reports which stretched the credulity of the British urban dweller almost to breaking point. The second was the careful monitoring of these disclosures by organizations such as the Royal Geographical Society and the Anthropological Institute, demonstrating a growing interest in the implications of such discoveries for the nature of humankind. The new disciplines of Archaeology and Anthropology, the rise of which coincided both with the revival of quest romance and with the high age of British imperialism, also had important literary consequences.[11] Lang, for instance, wrote Anthropology as well as folk tales. The adventure romances of his contemporaries, moreover, had this in common with empire-building: they laid stress on hard, practical know-how, and they led into regions of the earth and mind which were unsettling and, from a comfortable bourgeois point of view, decidedly strange.

The writers included in this study were all enthusiasts for the exotic and recondite – latter-day Casaubons or Lydgates swotting obscure branches of knowledge. They also loved hard, technical know-how, and the jargon which went with it. Stevenson, who was descended from a long line of engineers, was obsessed with maps, navigation, and boat-building; from his earliest years in Edinburgh, he also revelled in the technical details of stage-craft: scenery, lighting, and props. Haggard delved into comparative anthropology and Egyptology, a fascination with which was the basis of his friendship with Lang. A mock-Egyptian shard, made for him by his sister-in-law, set off his most famous romance *She*, and Haggard himself made frequent trips to excavations along the Nile. Throughout his adult life, he wore around the middle finger of his right hand a cumbersome brass ring dug up at the site of the shrine of Osiris at Abydos: it was said once to have graced the hand of Pharaoh Amenhotep's consort, Queen Nefertiti. For preference he read fact rather than novels, and spent much of later life investigating, and writing about, effective methods of agriculture and husbandry.

Kipling, too, was an inveterate student of the more abstruse sciences: of horticulture, agriculture, sanitation, and military history. Since his days working in India in his twenties, he had been fascinated by the terminology of closed societies. In his autobiographical essay *Something of Myself* he recalled how as a young journalist in Lahore in the 1880s he would spend hours at the local Punjab club, where 'I met none except picked men at their definite work – Civilians, Army, Education, Canals, Forestry, Engineering, Irrigation, Railways, Doctors and Lawyers – samples of each branch and each talking his own shop' (*SOM* 43). Ever afterwards Rudyard retained the temperament of a reporter; he was never happier than when swapping technical know-how, or overhearing professional small talk. Later, he grew obsessed with cars, graduating from a steam-powered Locomobile to a Lanchester, and eventually to Rolls Royces, taking relish in the inner workings of each vehicle: the jargon of workshop and road.

Conan Doyle was a medical graduate, whose interest in forensic science fed into his Sherlock Holmes stories. He devoted the closing years of his life to the practice and teaching of Spiritualism, of the authenticity of which he was deeply convinced. Indeed, the closer a branch of enquiry was to the suspect or bogus, the more interested in it he apparently became. In the last decade of his life, he was famously gulled by some rigged-up photographs into believing in the existence of fairies, a subject on which he wrote a perfectly serious book.[12] For Conan Doyle, the evidence suggested that pixies were actual beings; to track them down, even at the risk of ridicule, was an intellectual challenge, possessing its own kind of romance.

The attraction of such esoteric subjects for these writers was that they were both enjoyable and obscure, and could be discussed within a tightly knit, specialist peer group. It is far from coincidental that the revival of quest romance coincides with the emergence towards the end of the nineteenth century of the cult of the specialist or the 'expert'. It is also far from irrelevant that this cult coincides with a burgeoning of Freemasonry in the English-speaking world, Kipling, for instance, having been received into the Hope and Perseverance Lodge at Lahore in January 1885, in a bizarre ritual for which the hall was decorated with hangings 'after the prescription of Solomon's Temple' (*SOM* 52). Not merely is Freemasonry a male preserve; with its Egyptian symbolism, its ornate and fraternal rituals, its jealously guarded secrets, it is also a paradigm for particular kinds of arcane or occult information-gathering. A parallel may be drawn between the traditions of a Masonic lodge and the self-regulation of a college, or of a scientific or pseudo-scientific community. All these groupings rejoice in titles and exclusive modes of dress; all develop and maintain a technical language which leaves outsiders at a loss. In other words, all are closed societies for whom integration into the world at large matters less than the defence of a specialized brand of expertise, the cohesion of a self-regarding clique.

The groups of male travellers who feature in quest romances of this period represent, or rapidly become, closed societies of this kind, possessing their own rituals, argot, and jokes: in one of the stories by Kipling that I shall consider the common bond is actually Masonic. Though the adventurers are usually amateurs – indeed often pride themselves on being such – the nature of their enquiries has to do with the harnessing of technical and exclusive disciplines: Archaeology; Anthropology; Criminology; Theosophy; Egyptology; Navigation; Cartography; Palaeontology; Chemistry, Toxicology; engineering, and stagecraft to name only the most prominent. In most instances, the consummation of the quest consists of the verification of some factual, as opposed to moral, truth. In most of these stories the information thus acquired is the property of another closed society, whose unique possession of it must be violated and broken down in the process.

It is this process of assiduous assimilation that reminds Edward Said of domination; it is the deliberate cohesion of the investigative team that is responsible for the homosociality which the feminist Elaine Showalter is so keen to point out. In supplementing Said's account, however, we must add that the power relations in these stories are more ambiguous than he suggests. Likewise, in response to Showalter we must assert that the male bonding in such stories is both enriching and humorous. The response to female sexuality in these books, moreover, is more delighted and positive than Showalter's angle of approach leads her to suppose.

One fascinating question remains. Are the esoteric enquiries conducted by these groups of men mere whims of specialized curiosity, or do they amount to an attempt to decipher some larger, inclusive mystery? A close look at the books themselves will, I think, suggest that the questions troubling these bands of seekers all resolve themselves into one overriding quest.

3

Beyond the Lighthouse: Stevenson's *Treasure Island*

In the late 1870s Webb's theatrical print shop in Old Street, London, was in the habit of receiving visits from a tall, thin, tubercular Scotsman. The shop, run by father and son, was cramped, and from the lintel of the entrance hung play sheets, engraved by the proprietors, costing a penny if black and white, and twopence if coloured. The customer, Robert Louis Stevenson, appreciated both kinds. Years afterwards H. J. Webb, the son of the shop's founder, recalled one of those visits: 'as he [Stevenson] came in he noticed some of the coloured sheets hanging in the doorway, and at once struck a theatrical attitude ... He used to talk Toy Theatres by the hour with my father.'[1] Another recipient of these visits was Benjamin Pollock, who maintained a similar establishment near Shoreditch. Pollock noticed how tall Stevenson's slender body appeared, since he constantly bumped his head on the ceiling when entering the premises. He noted too the contrast between his customer's consumptive appearance – 'his hands were so thin,' he once observed, 'you could almost see through them' – and the obvious relish that he displayed for the activities of highwaymen and pirates.

Stevenson's fascination with the juvenile drama went back to his childhood home at 17, Heriot Row, Edinburgh, where he received a Skelt's model theatre for his sixth birthday. From a shop in Leith Walk he had purchased play sheets to act out in this gift with carefully cut-out and glued-together figures. At the rear of its miniature stage he had suspended backdrops, often depicting the sea. In 'A Penny Plain and Twopence Coloured', an article which appeared in the *Magazine of Art* in April 1884, he left an unforgettable account of the impact of 'this cut-and-dry, dull, swaggering, obtrusive and infantile art' on an impressionable, sickly child. For Stevenson, toy theatres held a double attraction. First, they were intensely practical playthings, which the child was obliged to construct, following detailed instructions, and then to operate sometimes single-handed, turning himself into director, stage manager, lighting technician and actor in one. Secondly, their sets, like Keats's casement from 'Ode to a Nightingale', gave onto 'fairy lands forlorn'. The main indication as to the location of each scene was its cardboard backdrop: sometimes of a ship, sometimes of a castle or palace (as in *Aladdin*, a favourite piece for toy theatre addicts), often of a desert island or the ocean. 'Blackbeard the Pirate', adapted for miniature theatres at least four times, was set entirely aboard *The Revenge*.[2]

The twin appeal of practicality and romance was always to exert a strong pull upon Stevenson. His engineer father Thomas had erected lighthouses in the Shetlands, and his father before him had set up the Bell Rock Lighthouse in the Firth of Forth. Louis had himself been intended for this family profession. It was as an engineering student that he had matriculated at Edinburgh University in 1867, winning a silver medal from the Edinburgh Society of Arts four years later for the design of a lighthouse beacon. He soon forsook engineering for law, and then literature. The joint appeal of practical know-how, and of marine locations, however, never released its hold. Struck down by tuberculosis in his twenties, his self-prescribed restorative was to travel far and wide, and always in the most gruelling circumstances: by canal boat through France and Belgium; by donkey through the Cevennes mountains; by emigrant ship and train to San Francisco; finally by schooner yacht to Samoa. These journeys were all attempts at a cure, and ways of escape from dark, cold, Presbyterian Scotland, of which the influence on him was nevertheless always strong.[3] In Stevenson we are confronted with a unique and powerful combination of invalidism and Celtic wanderlust.

The origin of *Treasure Island* (1883), Stevenson's best-known work, is inseparably connected with his reading in traditional romances. In 1878 he immersed himself in what was to become a standard source of late-nineteenth-century romantic fantasy, *The*

Arabian Nights. A vogue for these oriental tales was later to be inspired by Richard Burton's English translation of 1885–8. Stevenson, however, read them in the French translation by Anton Galland, and was soon busy writing a series of modern tales along the same lines, first published in W. E. Henley's weekly paper, *London* and issued in book form in 1882 as *The New Arabian Nights*. He spent the previous summer at Braemar in the Highlands with his parents, his wife Fanny, and his 12-year-old step-son Lloyd. The weather was abysmal, and Stevenson in poor health. To offset the tedium, he began telling the boy a yarn involving pirates and lost booty, called initially *The Ship's Cook*.

The idea for the story apparently originated with a map that Lloyd had been doodling with his paintbox, and which Stevenson helped him complete.[4] According to the dedication page, it was tailor-made to the boy's 'classic taste' – that is, to his love for traditional romantic tales. Its unique atmosphere, however, is the result of two ingenious elements: the insertion of the child's own consciousness at the heart of the narrative, and the careful recreation, via a welter of historical and technical detail, of the seafaring life of the Hanoverian period in which it is set.

Like Stevenson himself, the book's hero Jim Hawkins is an only child. Like Lloyd, who had spent the previous few years travelling around with Stevenson and Fanny, he is also isolated from the company of other children, who are notably absent throughout the tale. Though Jim's parents make a fleeting appearance at the beginning, his father soon dies, and his mother is conveniently settled where he can reach her after his adventures are over. As soon as the quest for the treasure is set in motion by the discovery of Billy Bones's map, he enters a society exclusively composed of male adventurers, drawn from the professional class, the squirearchy, and from seamen of various ranks, law abiding or otherwise.

The book thus caters to a young man's desire to enter a peer group of his elders, and to be treated by them as an equal. The story enacts an induction into a world of adult social arrangements, dispensing with age distinctions and bonding with a hierarchical society of energetic men. Purportedly, Captain Flint's buried treasure is the object of the quest. When it is finally discovered, safely stowed in Ben Gunn's cave on the island, its appearance, however, seems almost anticlimactic. Jim is remarkably uninformative as to how to spend his share. One reason for this omission may be that by the end of the story the boy has achieved the real object of his personal quest: the respect and reliance of his elders. The other reason is that the spending of money is a landlubbing tale; and *Treasure Island* is overwhelmingly concerned with the dispensation of the sea.

The novel begins in a cove on the Devon coast, and much of it happens on the island itself, which seems to be situated slightly to the west of Trinidad. Throughout, however, the defining society is that of shipboard. The schooner *Hispaniola* is a floating male society, nominally governed by its captain Smollet, whose name irresistibly recalls the eighteenth-century author of picaresque novels such as *Peregrine Pickle*. It is only when they set sail that the social composition and line-up of Jim's companions, and the peculiar criss-cross of their personal allegiances, make themselves felt. At the very outset, their differences spell themselves out territorially, the hired seaman insisting on occupying the fore of the ship, leaving the stern to the captain, the squire, and the doctor. It is this physical arrangement of the crew, and also of the provisions, that first alerts the captain to the possibility of a mutiny. As soon as they arrive, moreover, Treasure Island itself turns into a duplicate ship: with its three mountain tops – 'Foremast Hill', 'Spyglass Hill', and 'Missenmast Hill' – standing for the masts on deck. The stockade at the south end of the island is placed in exactly the same position as the captain's quarters on the schooner, immediately before the missen hill or mast – that is, figuratively behind the wheelhouse. Appropriately enough, it is in the 'blockhouse' at the centre of this clearing that Captain Smollet sets up his headquarters, arranging it internally very much like his cabin aboard the *Hispaniola*, and flying the Union Jack from the roof. The buccaneers, in the meantime, situate themselves further to the north, in an area of the terrain equivalent, in nautical terms, to the foc's'le.

The polarization thus achieved, however, soon turns out to be as provisional as it was on the ship. Nominally, the two groups are opposed to one another, since the captain's party, who are initially in possession of the only complete chart of the island, are determined to keep Captain Flint's treasure out of the hands of the pirates. This neat distinction of jurisdiction and morality, however, quickly breaks down. First – though, in his wonderment, Jim does not disclose this – the squire Trelawney, the doctor, and the captain are no more entitled to the booty than are the buccaneers. Indeed, since the pirates are former colleagues of the Captain Flint who buried the booty in the first place, their claim would seem to be stronger than that of the lawgivers. Trelawney bases his claim to the treasure on his legal status in England; in this exotic setting, however, this argument carries as little weight as it does in the eyes of the reader.

Secondly, we cannot help noticing that, though their interests are at odds, the captain's party and the pirates respect very much the same conventions. Ragged and drunken they may be, but Silver and his conspirators are still a crew, and pay constant lip-service to nautical protocol. As Jim rapidly discovers, to earn the respect of either party, he has to sing very much the same tune. Both groups, for example, survive by their wits, and each builds up an intense camaraderie based on rivalry, competition, and the arts of survival. In this world, right and wrong hardly signify; though some characters are villains, and others possess a capacity for heroism, the most interesting are morally ambiguous. Long John Silver, pre-eminently, is neither rogue nor hero, but a strange compound of bluster, deviousness, and compassion. Were he a more straightforward man he would forfeit the sympathy of Jim, and the interest of the reader as well. Indeed, though Silver changes sides, not once but twice, his versatility does not, I think, ever offend us, or even compromise him in our eyes.

The reason for our suspension of judgement is that the quest itself is morally void. The point of the journey is not to win, or even to prove a point: it is to play. Indeed it would be absurd to interpret this quest for illegal booty as any kind of a mission. As a result, the avarice of the leading players is not simply exonerated; it becomes neutral, a sort of blind empirical force.

In this isolated and regimented company of desperadoes, two factors alone count. The first is practical resourcefulness; the second is obedience to an unwritten but universally recognized code. The first of these may escape the attention of readers unfamiliar with nautical lore. It is, however, important to realize that, not only in *Treasure Island,* but in the male quest romances to which it gave rise, the skill and *savoir-faire* of each character is of paramount importance. In a social realist novel set in London or Manchester, the tools and jargon of a trade merely add colour. In a quest romance, by contrast, a grasp of practicalities is the basis of mutual respect. In the risky circumstances such as these stories describe, reliability of a practical sort bears a deeper significance than civility, or even ethics. Jim, for example, soon outwears his cachet as ship's junior; thenceforth he has to prove his worth by being useful. It is as a result of his skilful eavesdropping in the apple barrel that he is first admitted to the inner circle of the captain's cabin. His ultimate acceptance as an equal comes when he stealthily releases the *Hispaniola* from its anchor and steers it to a more accessible berth on the north shore of the island. The respect that he gains from the captain, the doctor, and the squire as a result of this escapade stems less from his initiative than from his ability to perform so difficult a physical manœuvre.

The second relevant criterion of merit, the unwritten code, is also strongly related to practical effectiveness. It would be easy to misrepresent it as a set of rules designed to safeguard the hierarchy. Discipline in the conventional sense, however, is difficult to maintain on the island. Instead, law and order are replaced by a network of recognizable though informal obligations. From that point on, the statute book plays the same kind of role in the matrix of social relations as a ground bass might in a piece of music, or bar lines in a hornpipe. In other words, it exists as a backdrop for improvisation.

In part five of the book, for example, Jim slips out of the log house when the attentions of his companions are elsewhere. He thinks of this metaphorical act of slipping ship as an instance of 'insubordination'; he is quite well aware that he should *in theory* have asked Smollet's permission before absconding. In practice, and not for the first time, his impetuosity saves the expedition. When his superiors eventually realize that he has rescued their skins, they neglect to reprimand him for disobedience, since he has so evidently acted for the common good. Their reaction is quite consistent with the values enunciated by the book as a whole. Stevenson, one remembers, was himself in reaction against the constricting uniformity of his Calvinist background.

Abstract ethics meant as little to him as, in this tale, they do to the sailors. Stevenson, furthermore, was a member of a generation schooled by the essays of Ralph Waldo Emerson, with their emphasis on 'impulse'. To act spontaneously for the well-being of one's fellows, even in the face of the rules, was the very essence of his code.

Thus, in the quasi-naval setting of Treasure Island, behaviour is assessed less against the rules than against one supreme value: duty or, as Silver pronounces it, 'dooty'. This term derives from a Latin word for to owe, and is obliquely connected with customs tariffs. Smugglers, for example, are defined as people who import or export goods without paying the authorities what they owe them; by this token, they could be said to be guilty of 'dereliction of duty'. On Treasure Island the pirates do not consider that they owe anything to Trelawney and his cronies; they therefore regard themselves as being released from any obligation to them. Yet their own *esprit de corps* vitally depends on a sense of interdependence quite as binding as that which unites the captain's party. In that sense, the two groups mirror one another. As Jim soon finds out, the respectability or otherwise of those with whom he has to deal is less important than cohesion enforced by this utilitarian notion of 'duty'. When he finally reaches the stockade after his nocturnal adventure, he finds Silver's party newly in possession. The presiding values should thus in theory have been turned upside down. When Silver jokingly upbraids him for his conduct, however, he soon discovers that this is far from the case:

> Now, you see, Jim, so be as you *are* here,' says he, 'I'll give you a piece of my mind. I've always liked you, I have, for a lad of spirit, and a picter of my own self when I was young and handsome. I always wanted you to jine and take your share, and die a gentleman, and now, my cock, you've got to. Cap'n Smollet's a fine seaman, as I'll own up to any day, but stiff on discipline. "Dooty is dooty," says he, and right he is. Just you keep clear of the cap'n. The doctor himself is gone dead clean again you – "ungrateful scamp" was what he said; and the short and the long of the whole story is about here: you can't go back to your own lot, for they won't have you; and, without you start a third ship's company all by yourself, which might be lonely, you'll have to jine with Cap'n Silver.' (*TI* 150)

A great many feelings are blended into this colloquy: affection, muffled aggression, needling persuasiveness, avuncular charm. Silver acts towards his young friend in much the way in which an elder brother treats his younger, or the Akela of a cub-scout pack treats a promising and high-spirited 'sixer', or a bully his victim, or a boss treats a young employee he happens to have taken a shine to. They like one another, they speak the same language; because of what they share, they can do business, even if they are enemies. Male bonding is at work here in a particularly efficient way. Silver knows what it is like to be Jim, and, within limits, Jim can interpret Silver's signals. Indeed, so complete is this empathy that Jim's own narrative momentarily inflects into Silver's register, echoing his idiomatic use of the historic present: '"so be as you *are* here", says he.' The ironic, drawling emphasis on the verb 'are' carries much of Silver's meaning, which amounts to this: discipline, loyalty, and friendship are fine things, but, seeing as you have placed yourself in this invidious position, deal with the situation that exists and forget about the rest. The force of this argument is so strong that Jim, whose affinity with Silver is clear throughout the book, half accepts it: at least as far as playing along until such times as the doctor turns up on his errand of mercy to the wounded. This half resolve remains true, despite the fact that Jim recognizes that Silver is lying: the captain and the squire would never desert him, even if Silver plays on his fears that they might. Silver presses his case by appealing to the very values of allegiance that they both hold dear. A feeling for the clique divides them, but in the present predicament it can also bring them together. Silver pays Jim the ultimate compliment: he invites him to 'jine'.

The scene is set towards the end of the story, and in a way represents the apogee of Jim's fortunes: vulnerable as he is, Silver is playing for his trust. The reason Jim accepts the offer is that he is able to see through Silver's bluff, and to realize that the old sea dog is actually in a far more extreme plight than himself. Jim has come a long way from the boy in the 'Admiral Benbow' inn who cringed at the very sight of Blind Pew. If we were talking about a social realist novel, we might infer that he has 'grown up' or 'come to maturity'. But this is romance, and Jim has acquired something far more serviceable than moral awareness: he has learned the rules of the game. He has not lost his youth as a result, or even really quit childhood. Stevenson has nothing in him of the Romantic obsession with infancy and its loss: we are not in the Neverland of Sir James Barry's Peter Pan. Instead I would argue that Jim has exchanged one sort of innocence – based on wide-eyed curiosity – for another variety, based on cooperation and zest.

It is worthwhile dwelling on *Treasure Island* because in many ways it is the founding text in the revival of quest romance. Stevenson, of course, wrote many other romances, some of which fall obliquely within our genre. In the finest of them, the historical romance *Kidnapped* (1886), an adolescent boy is tricked by his avaricious and domineering uncle into embarking on a voyage to the Carolinas. His capture leads to shipwreck and ironically sets him free to explore, first the hinterland of Scotland, and secondly his own delighted sense of self-determination. Again the story enacts a rite of passage in which the protagonist's personal identity, intimately connected with the arts of mere survival, is the real object of the quest. In *The Strange Case of Dr Jekyll and Mr Hyde* (also 1886), the act of emancipation is realized within the personality of one character who, by performing crimes beyond the pale of civilized society, eludes at one and the same time the claims of respectability and his own censorious self. This theme of doubleness, which Stevenson may have owed to an anterior Scottish text, James Hogg's *Confessions of a Justified Sinner* (1824), recurs in *The Master of Ballantrae* (1889), where the division is between two brothers who project reverse images of one another. In *The Weir of Hermiston*, posthumously published in 1896, the beneficent and malign aspects of Calvinism stare one another out in the persons of a cruel, repressive judge and his idealistic son.

In all of these books, however, there is a strict divide between the acceptable face of morality (Dr Jekyll) and the repressed and juxtaposed anarchy of the individual (Mr Hyde). Mr Hyde is brought to justice; the miserly uncle in *Kidnapped* succumbs. The enduring popularity of *Treasure Island*, I think, owes much to the fact that in it Stevenson forgets the nagging conflict between Good and Evil and introduces us to a toy-theatre world, familiar to the unconscious mind of all its readers, which is amoral rather than immoral. The real treasure, in fact, is the pre-moral nature of man, the drives that actually motivate, as opposed to supposedly motivate, men and women, in their private and social behaviour. The sailors can realize these drives in their naked state only by leaving England. The island is the place where you can be your pre-moral, piratical self. Because the book is apparently aimed at children, and is technically a romance, Stevenson gets away with this anti-moral moral, as he could scarcely have done while writing a novel. The book's success is that it takes us back to that part of ourselves, exercised to the full before each of us learned to behave, in which we are all that irresistible and irresponsible 'ships's cook', Long John Silver.

4

Rider Haggard's African Romances

In the spring of 1885 Henry Rider Haggard, then the author of a book about Zululand and an ineffectual novel called *Dawn*, was travelling up to Liverpool Street Station from his home in Norfolk. Opposite him in the train compartment sat his elder brother John, a former naval officer. In her biography of Rider, Lilias Haggard, the writer's daughter, catches the swaggering tone of their conversation: 'they started discussing *Treasure Island*. Rider said he didn't think that it was so very remarkable, whereupon his brother replied, rather indignantly: "Well, I'd like to see you write anything half as good – bet you a bob you can't." "Done." said Rider ....'.[1]

It is much in the spirit of Haggard's fiction that he should have embarked on the writing of travel romance in response to a wager. As a matter of fact, he respected Stevenson's work deeply, though typically his reaction was to attempt to beat the Scottish author at his own game. In his autobiography *The Days of my Life* he makes this spirit of competition perfectly clear. He also suggests that his plan to outdo Stevenson had been in his mind for some time. About 1882 he confessed, 'I read in one of the weekly papers a notice of Stevenson's *Treasure Island* so laudatory that I procured and studied that work, and was impelled by its perusal to write a book for boys' (*DML* i. 230). The result was *King Solomon's Mines*.

In setting off into this unknown literary territory, Haggard possessed one supreme advantage. Ten years previously, despairing of Rider's poor performance at school, his father had obtained for him a post on the staff of Sir Henry Bulwer, Lieutenant-Governor of the province of Natal in South Africa. In

Natal, Rider had discovered a new aptitude for work; he had impressed his superiors, learned Zulu, and helped to investigate a spate of witch persecutions then afflicting the province. Soon he had attracted the attention of the Secretary for Native Affairs, Sir Theophilus Shepstone, whom he accompanied on an expedition to annexe the Boer Transvaal in 1877. Rider had helped hoist the Union Jack in Pretoria; and shortly afterwards had been appointed Master and Registrar of the High Court of Justice at the age of 21. In 1879, as the Zulus rose under Chaka's great-nephew Cetywayo, inflicting heavy loses on the British, he had briefly served with the Pretoria Cavalry. When Garnet Wolseley, the draconian conqueror of Ashanti, was sent out from England to restore order at short notice, Haggard had watched in dismay as Cetywayo was replaced by a punch of puppet chieftains. Whilst on leave in Norfolk he had married, then returned to South Africa to farm. He had witnessed the First Boer War of 1880–1 end in victory for the Boers; the treaty restoring self-government to the Transvaal had been drafted in his farmhouse. Returning to England, he had studied for the bar, and in 1882 had published a non-fictional work entitled *Cetywayo and his White Neighbours, or Remarks on Recent Events in Zululand, Natal and Transvaal,* defending African polygamy, and bitterly attacking both the missionaries and the terms of Wolseley's settlement. 'Did we', he pleaded, 'owe nothing to this people whose kingdom we had broken up, and whom we had been shooting down by the thousands? They may well ask, as they do continually, what they have done that we should treat them as we have and are doing' (*C.* 38).[2] The book made little impact, but it gave Haggard confidence, in both his style and his judgement. It also conveyed the strong mixture of admiration and prejudice through which he viewed the indigenous cultures of Africa. Though possessed of the standard paternalistic prejudices of his age, he clearly had a healthy respect both for Cetywayo, noting 'how good, how big, how beautiful he is' (*C.* 2), and for the Zulu impis, who during his time in South Africa had crushed the British at Isandhlwana. In constructing his own brand of romance, Rider had therefore simply to expand on his experiences. Rhodes had not yet interfered with the peoples of the hinterland such as the Mashona and the Matabele. Southern Africa thus presented to Haggard's imagination a combination of familiar ground and *terra incognita*. In trying his hand at quest romance, he could now probe the – to him – unknown interior in his mind, while drawing on his own partial knowledge.

Haggard also possessed a keen amateur interest in what we would now call Social Anthropology, some of which he had read in connection with his legal work in South Africa. In the March of 1885 he had met Andrew Lang, whose recently published *Custom and Myth* (1884) he was soon dipping into, along with other works of comparative ethnology, such as Edward Burnett Tylor's *Primitive Culture*.[3] He was well aware, for example, that among the Zulus the names of former chiefs were tabooed for generations – an observation that he could only have picked up first hand, or else from an exceedingly obscure treatise published in Edinburgh in 1875. He also knew that Zulu kings preferred to be slain in single combat rather than to die of old age, and made sure to include a mock-learned footnote to this effect in his new book. Indeed, though he accepted that his talent was for spinning tales rather than for generalizing about other cultures, there was always a part of him that longed to be a scholar of custom and belief. He would indulge, and also poke fun at, this ponderous *alter persona* by slyly insinuating him into the text of successive suspenseful yarns.

His self-appointed task in 1885, however, was to write a book for boys. Rejecting Stevenson's ploy of inserting a child's consciousness into the text, he decided instead to create a fictional narrator called Allan Quatermain, as unlike himself as possible. At the time Rider himself was still in his twenties: tall, affable, and somewhat magisterial in manner. Quatermain would be in late middle age, diminutive, and almost pathologically modest. Rider had spent his short professional life as a bureaucrat and student of the law. His chosen narrator, by contrast, has devoted twenty years to hunting elephants. Rider had already proved himself a capable administrator, and was to become an accomplished after-dinner speaker; he designed Quatermain to be bumbling to the point of hilarity, saved from farce only by a fortunate streak of luck and practical good sense.

Rider was blessed with a fine constitution and good health. Though his constitution is 'wiry', Quatermain wears false teeth, and makes no attempt to hide his ineffectiveness in every physical pursuit apart from hunting. Rider was no intellectual;

he was, however, an omnivorous reader. Consequently, he denies his protagonist all knowledge of literature apart from the Revd Richard Barham's exercise in the Gothic grotesque, *The Ingoldsby Legends* (1840), which Quatermain quotes to himself in compromising situations, and scraps of poetry which are always drifting into his disorganized mind, without him being able to identify their sources. Rider habitually wrote with unpretentious panache and directness; Quatermain is a stylistic bumbler, whose principal figure of speech is a clumsy *meiosis* or understatement. Author and protagonist were to complement one another, to play tricks on one another, to enjoy themselves in ways that have delighted generations of schoolboys but which are invisible, apparently, to many professional critics.

In *King Solomon's Mines*, Quatermain is placed at the centre of an ill-sorted trio. While travelling by steamer from Elizabethville to Durban, he falls in with two vivid personalities as different from himself as they are unlike their creator. Captain John Good is a retired naval officer: bluff, humorous, and honourable, of middling height and dapper in appearance. Quatermain admires his false teeth, which are of an exceptional whiteness and evenness, fitting far better than his own. He is also much taken with Good's stylish collection of monocles.

Good is accompanied by Sir Henry Curtis, an English aristocrat from a stately home in Yorkshire. Classically educated, he is over six foot in height, blond, and straightforward in speech and manner. Curtis possesses all the refinements of gentlemanly courtesy, but is eaten up with remorse for having cheated his younger brother George out of an inheritance. Having heard that George has set off to investigate King Solomon's diamond mines in the interior, he hires Quatermain to assist him, promising him a large share of the diamonds, to whose whereabouts they possess a rough guide in the shape of an old Portuguese map.

Throughout the book Curtis, who has Danish blood in his veins, serves as an exemplar of Aryan physical perfection, who is treated by Quatermain with the deference of a new boy for a senior prefect. His height and bearing, moreover, are advantages which he shares both with the Zulus on the coast, and with the related ethnic group through whose territory they pass: the Kukuanas – a fictitious ethnic group who, however, have something in common with the Matabeles in what was later to become Rhodesia. Before the companions set out, they hire the services of a Zulu called Umbopa (named, incidentally, after Chaka's assassin) who is as fine a physical specimen of African, as Curtis is of British, manhood. The meeting of the two men is instructive:

> Sir Henry told me to ask him to stand up. Umbopa did so, at the same time slipping off the long military coat which he wore, and revealing himself naked except for the moocha around his centre and a necklace of lions' claws. Certainly he was a magnificent-looking man; I never saw a finer native. Standing about six foot three high he was broad in proportion, and very shapely. In that light, too, his skin looked scarcely more than dark, except here and there where deep black scars marked old assegai wounds. Sir Henry walked up to him and looked into his proud, handsome face.
>
> 'They make a good pair, don't they?' said Good; 'one as big as the other.'
>
> 'I like your looks, My Umbopa, and I will take you as my servant', said Sir Henry in English.
>
> Umbopa evidently understood him, for he answered in Zulu, 'It is well'; and then added, with a glance at the white man's great stature and height, 'We are men, thou and I.' (*KSM* 48–9)

Many undercurrents run through this short scene. Curtis and Umbopa are equal in physical stature, though divided by race, rank, and language. In this tense instant of embarrassed mutual recognition, they seem to obliterate their companions. If, as Umbopa asserts with subdued pride, he and the English aristocrat are both 'men', what manner of creatures are the pint-sized Quatermain, and the unimpressive-looking Good? It is as if, just for a moment, the 'racism' of which Haggard's detractors sometimes accuse him is blotted out by a 'sizeism' that cuts right across the cultural and linguistic divide, sustaining this ill-matched pair of giants in a condition of uneasy Darwinian parity. The emotions which they betray as a result are such as have seldom been discussed by critics of colonial fiction. They range from self-satisfaction at being prize physical specimens of their respective groups to personal rivalry, and an instinctual sense of biological kinship transcending the colour line, yet hemmed in by it.

Their sense of shared superiority is further endorsed when

Umbopa, thenceforth known as 'Ignosi', is revealed as the usurped rightful heir to the throne of the Kukuanas. With this unexpected discovery, the barrier of status dividing him from Curtis disappears. Considering the date of the book, it would not have been surprising if the impact of this event had been eliminated by the remaining racial distinction between the two men. Surprisingly, however, though the cordon between European and 'native' is of paramount importance on the coast, once the action moves to the hinterland, racial taboos prove surprisingly weak. When, determined to oust Twala, the incumbent king of the Kukuanas, Umbopa decides to stage a pitched battle, the three Europeans are kitted out in suits of chainmail, lent to them by their local hosts. Curtis goes one further, and dons the regalia of a Kukuana warlord. 'The dress,' observes Quatermain with his characteristic blimpishness,

> was, no doubt, a savage one, but I am bound to say that I seldom saw a finer sight than Sir Henry Curtis presented in this disguise. It showed off his magnificent physique to the greatest advantage, and when Ignosi arrived presently, arrayed in a similar costume, I thought to myself that I had never before seen two such splendid men. (*KSM* 200)

In the ensuing battle, Curtis is placed at the head of the crack regiment of Kukuana veterans called the Greys. As he moves backwards and forwards among his troops, it is clear that he has, in Quatermain's eyes, been transformed into a white Zulu.

The impressive virility of Curtis's appearance has the peculiar effect of feminizing his two white companions. Quatermain, for one, is dwarfed by him, just as he is by Ignosi, Twala, and the entire Kukuana army. His reaction is pathetically to dance attendance on the larger man, deferring to him at vital moments, and seeking protection behind his strength. Quatermain's obsequiousness has the effect of exaggerating his natural diffidence, so that he paints himself as a physical coward: bashful, bumbling, prone to rushes of almost girlish modesty. The most demeaning transformation, however, occurs in the formally personable Good. With his false teeth and absurdly prominent monocle, the former naval officer is already marked by physical inferiority. These unprepossessing attributes are reduced to comic proportions by his obsessive fastidiousness and vanity. Forever folding his clothes and surreptitiously shaving, he is finally turned into a laughing stock when surprised at his ablutions by a Kukuana scouting party. Since he has removed his trousers, and one side of his face is unshaved, his white companions encourage the locals in the impression that his incomplete toilet is a sign of divinity. To sustain this hoax, he is obliged to enter the Kukuana capital, Loos, in risible *déshabillé*. His stark white legs attract first the curiosity, and then the lust, of the local girls. Good is a most unlikely sex symbol: passive, tongue-tied, in fact much like a stereotypical English maiden. None of the African males in this story, let it be stressed, is similarly compromised in the reader's eyes. Indeed, in the battle scene, the Kukuana veterans are compared by the narrator to the Cincinnati, the heroic defenders of ancient Rome. Ridicule, where it occurs, is reserved for the white men.

The inequality between the three Europeans in terms of personal resolve is epitomized by their reactions when, reaching the mines, they are immured within its innermost cave. Quatermain leans his head against Curtis's broad shoulder, while he and Good give way to tears:

> Ah, how good and brave that great man was! Had we been two frightened children, and he our nurse, he could not have treated us more tenderly. Forgetting his own share of miseries, he did all he could to soothe our broken nerves, telling stories of men who had been in somewhat similar circumstances, and miraculously escaped; and when these failed to cheer us, pointing out how, after all, it was only anticipating an end which must come to us all, that it would soon be over, and that death from exhaustion was a merciful one (which is not true). (*KSM* 288–9)

The incongruous blend of psychology and gender in Haggard's trio of explorers was too much for the producers of the most celebrated of the five film adaptations of *King Solomon's Mines*, made by Metro Goldwyn Meyer in 1950. They turned the diminutive Quatermain into a raven-haired six-footer, acted by Stewart Granger, and in place of Curtis provided him with a nubile redhead played by the curvaceous Deborah Kerr. At the same time they moved the action from southern Africa to Kenya, where memories of the recent Mau Mau atrocities had the effect of reducing the nobility of the Kukuanas, played by Masai extras, to an uncomplicated ferocity. It is important in this connection to realize that Haggard was writing against the background of early colonial intervention in Africa, whereas the producers of this film version were prompted by the *angst* of colonial withdrawal. The two moods are sufficiently different to remind us just how far the tone of Haggard's book is from the simpler pressures of twentieth-century propaganda.

Indeed, Haggard has a complex and sophisticated interest in his Kukuana creations, for reasons that become obvious when the three white men reach the mines. They are accompanied by Foulata, a beautiful Kukuana girl who has fallen in love with Good, and by the cadaverous Gagool, an aged crone who symbolizes the ageless memory of the Kukuana people. At the mouth of the cavern are posted three monumental statues known as the Silent Ones, whom Curtis identifies as the Phoenician divinities Astarte (Ashtoroth), Chemosh, and Milcom, mentioned in the Old Testament in 2 Kings 23: 13. The explorers then enter the mine via a cavernous antechamber dominated by a series of tall stalactites, formed over many centuries by silicous water dripping from the roof. In the adjoining chamber, a shock awaits them: round a table sit the bodies of the former rulers of Kukuanaland, with the decapitated corpse of the latest, Twana, squatting in their midst, his head clasped on his knee. The deceased kings have been petrified by the slow dripping of silicon from above. At the top of the table stands a skeleton wielding a sword, carved out of one large stalactite by an unknown hand.

The erect figure recalls Milton's 'Death' from *Paradise Lost*, but the other statues stir even older memories in the intruders, and potentially in the reader too. The macabre death-in-life of this tableau of one-time kings represents an entombed civilization, ossified by history into a bizarre condition of synchronous stasis. Together with the biblical figures at the entrance to the cave complex, they speak of a stage of culture common to all peoples: indeed, as the narrative makes clear, the mantle of ice by which the dead monarchs are covered has had the effect of *whitening* them. The extreme reactions evinced by the explorers, who are tempted at this point to take to their heels, are not those of men faced with alien presences, so much as of people confronted by an aspect of their own past that they dare not face. The frisson of this discovery, which resonates even through the title of the book, has to do with a process sometimes called *anamnesis*: the unveiling of facets of collective history which successive generations have wilfully suppressed. In staring at those gaunt, irresistible effigies trapped in their symbolic ice, Quatermain, Curtis, and Good are not assuaging academic curiosity about an exotic people. They are confronting spectres of *themselves*.

It is against the background of this moment of awareness that the remainder of Haggard's African trilogy must be viewed. The immediate sequel, *Allan Quatermain* (1887), supposedly written by the now 63-year-old elephant hunter in England three years after his account of his voyage among the Kukuanas, carries a Preface in which he rhetorically asks:

> Ah! this civilisation, what does it all come to? For forty years and more I lived among savages, and studied them and their ways; and now for several years I have lived here in England, and have in my own stupid manner done my best to learn the ways of the children of light; and what have I found? A great gulf fixed? No, only a very little one, that a plain man's thought may spring across. (*AQ* 10)

As if to illustrate this point, the second novel in the trilogy describes an expedition by Quatermain, Curtis, and Good to the interior of East Africa in search of a fabled white tribe. East Africa, let it be said, was a much less familiar region to Haggard than the south of the continent, and the Masai people among whom much of their route passes were less well known to him than the Zulus: for information on the Masai, for example, he is indebted partly to a book called *Through Masai Land*, published by Joseph Thomson a couple of years previously, and partly to the observations of his brother John, now Her Britannic Majesty's Consul in Madagascar.[4] Rider's lack of direct acquaintance with the country shows up in Quatermain's account of their safari, full of stock incidents and unsubtle characterization such as are by and large absent from the earlier book. The story comes to life only when they pass beyond 'Mount Kenia' (as Haggard spells Mount Kenya) to a region barely sketched on contemporary maps. Here Rider's anthropological grasp fails him completely, but he is forced to rely on something just as interesting: a projection onto the African interior of a kind of inverted, looking-glass England.

The fictitious country that they now enter is called 'Zu-Vendis' or 'Yellow Land'. It is significant that they make their incursion into it through a literal act of penetration. Through a half submerged tunnel, the travellers enter a broad, placid lake, on the shore of which stands the city of Melosis (in the Zu-Vendis language this name means 'the frowning city', though a Greek derivation would render it as 'honeyed'.) It is ruled by two beautiful twin sisters. The elder, Nyleptha, is blond and sympathetic; the junior, Sorais, dark-haired, stately, and peevish. As joint queens, they also share the role of 'Head of the Church', though the state religion, of course, is not Christianity but a form of sun worship. The family system, which is polygamous, unusually combines patrilinear with matrilinear descent: that is to say, the children of the first wife of a marriage are of 'the house of the father', while the offspring of all subsequent unions belong to the mother's kindred. Since women now occupy the throne, this ordinance now threatens the political stability of a country in which two taboos are rigorously enforced. The first of these is that the hippopotamus, revered as a sacred animal, should never be slain; the second and more sensitive is that a foreigner should not succeed to the throne. The all-important second stipulation is enshrined in a large slab of black marble placed in the palace courtyard which, should an 'outlander' ever become king, will irretrievably shatter.

The newcomers break each of these taboos in turn. On their arrival, Quatermain seeks to impress his hosts by shooting a hippo dead, for which crime he and his companions are condemned to be sacrificed to the sun god by the Chief Priest Agon, a malevolent Archbishop-of-Canterbury-like figure whose name suggests strife. At the last moment they are rescued from this fate by Nyleptha, who unfortunately puts the royal line at risk in the process by falling in love with the eligible Sir Henry, a situation rendered still more vexed when her sister falls for him as well. Civil war ensues.

Curtis believes that the Zu-Vendians, who are white, were originally Phoenicians, like the sculptors who once carved 'the Silent Ones' in Kukuanaland. Quatermain's alternative theory is that they were Persians who migrated from Babylon some centuries before Christ. The implications of this second view – which Haggard does not literally spell out – are suggestive, since the ancient Persians, like the Parsi community of present-day

Bombay, were Zoroastrians who worshipped fire, and who believed in the symbolic opposition of light and darkness. In the story these two principles seem to be embodied by the twin queens, one fair, the other dark. The younger of the two, moreover, who is constantly referred to as 'Sorais of Night', may remind some readers of the Queen of the Night in Mozart's *Magic Flute*. In any case, a battle follows in which, as in Mozart's opera, the forces of light prevail. Ominously for the national identity of Zu-Vendis, Nyleptha marries Curtis.

The more interesting parallels, however, are with Queen Victoria's England. The betrothal of Nyleptha and the teutonic Sir Henry irresistibly recalls the young Victoria's courting of Prince Albert, an already historic event which had been enshrined in the public memory, as in the monarch's heart, ever more firmly since the Consort's untimely death in 1861. Haggard portrays the Zu-Vendians as obsessed by a fear of what the anthropologists were just beginning to call 'exogamy': marriage outside the ethnic group. Politically regarded, the marriage of Victoria and Albert had been 'exogamous', even though Albert had been the English queen's first cousin. Exogamy, furthermore, was a hot topic among anthropologists at the time: Sir James Frazer, who had made an exhaustive study of the institution, wrote about it in his book on *Totemism*, published in the same year as *Allan Quatermain*, and was to make it central to the second and third editions of *The Golden Bough*. In Haggard's romance, the public threat of an exogamous union is represented by Curtis, whose explicit crowning as 'King Consort' thus represents a sort of conquest by stealth. Towards the end of the book, Quatermain listens to Agon's anxieties about the consequences of royal children being born of a foreign father, especially about the possibility of an alien religion eventually being imposed on the country. When Agon asks him which is the established faith in England, 'I told him that so far as I could remember, we had ninety-five different ones' (*AQ* 225).

Issued in the year of the Golden Jubilee, *Allan Quatermain* thus draws on deep-seated worries and contradictions in the Victorian mind: about the validity of conquest, about national identity, and about the role of men in a country which had now been ruled by a woman for exactly half a century. Throughout, for example, it is the females who do the wooing. When the travellers first reach Zu-Vendis, the country is in effect a matriarchy; Curtis's eventual accession as King Consort ensures a reversion to the patrilinear and patriarchal norm. All of these concerns surface again, far more powerfully, in the third and most successful of Haggard's African romances: *She*.

Ludwig Horace Holly, the donnish narrator of *She*, has this much in common with Quatermain: he is small, physically ill-favoured, and seemingly sexually isolated. He also resembles Quatermain in his somewhat wearisome insistence on his own shortcomings. In every other respect he is contrasted: wise, erudite, the Fellow a Cambridge college, learned in Latin and Greek literature, salting his account with a dry, unobtrusive wit.

In one respect, furthermore, Holly is a living anomaly. Swarthy, beetle-browed, hairy, his physical appearance irresistibly reminds his acquaintances of a monkey. He makes no bones about this, interpreting it with typical intellectual honesty as the reason for his reclusive, misanthropic character. Women flee from him. One week before the beginning of the story, he tells us, 'I had heard one call me a "monster", when she thought I was out of hearing, and say that I had converted her to the monkey theory' (*S.* 8) This, of course, is a straight reference to Darwin's theory of evolution as expounded in *The Origin of Species* (1859) and, more pertinently, in *The Descent of Man* (1871). In his physical person, Holly is the walking proof of the hypothesis of mankind's simian origins. Mentally a type of intellectual refinement, bodily he is a degenerate – one, that is, who, far from climbing up the ladder of being, has dramatically reverted to the brute.

The perverse conjunction of these two conditions endows Holly with poignancy and asperity, influencing his account decisively. Unlike the two previous books, *She* makes no pretence to be an adventure story for boys, but is a multifaceted discourse aimed at sophisticated adult readers with their burden of expectation, doubt, curiosity, and querulousness. The one function that it does not fulfil, *pace* some of its commentators, is that of unmediated compensatory fantasy.

Because the text is a more complex one than its predecessors, we receive it by a far less direct route. The Allan Quatermain books had purported to be direct, unadorned testimonies of real-life happenings. Indeed, so ingenuous had Quatermain himself been, so dismissive of literary pretension, that the readers were never tempted to look behind his words, or to question the epistemological standing of his narrative. *She*, by contrast, comes to us, not from its narrator, but from an anonymous editor who has been entrusted with the publication of Holly's manuscript, the author himself having in the meantime absconded to Tibet for further escapades with his irrepressible young ward, Leo Vincy. Appropriately, therefore, the text carries two different sets of footnotes: one written by Holly, crammed with scholarly glosses, parallels, and allusions (Lang may very well have assisted Haggard with this set), the other, far more pedestrian, compiled by the editor himself, full of general observations on the reliability of the manuscript and its relevance to the reader's supposed needs. Both forms of annotation serve as elaborations around, as well as displacements of, the main thrust of the text, which thus comes to us beset with a series of provisos. The insertion of this matter is another of Haggard's notorious literary jokes. Not only does *She* purvey a mystery; it offers us a declaration, penned by a narrator-in-hiding.

The central mystery itself concerns the reading of a text, or rather of texts. Soon after putting in for a fellowship at his college, Holly is entrusted by a fellow student called M. L. Vincy with a casket, and with the responsibility of bringing up his 5-year-old son, Leo. Leo, we gather, was born to Vincy by his late lamented Greek wife, who died in the act of childbirth. The child is being looked after in the country somewhere; if Ludwig accepts the terms of this commission, Vincy will leave enough money for him to bring up the boy, and hire domestic help for the purpose. The casket will be placed in the vaults of a London bank, and on the boy's twenty-fifth birthday be opened in front of him, since its contents vitally concern him. Accepting the terms, Holly hires a phlegmatic individual called Job as a manservant, moves out of his college rooms, and arranges to meet the boy. When Leo has grown into a personable twenty-five year old, the casket is retrieved, and its contents examined. They consist of an Egyptian potsherd of the third century BC bearing a Greek inscription purportedly in the hand of Amenertas, wife of Vincy's linear ancestor, Kallikretes, once Priest of the goddess Isis.

The text on sherd is presented to us with a set of

transliterations and translations. Holly himself renders the original uncial into cursive Greek, and then gives us Vincy's English translation. There are also testimonials from various of Vincy's forebears, telling us about the survival and presentation of the sherd. Despite this accumulated evidence, the story which the inscription tells is one that Holly has no hesitation in dismissing as spurious. It describes the migration of Kallikretes and Amenertas to the coast of Central Africa, where they encounter a civilization ruled over by an enigmatic and stately Arabic queen. This comely monarch, the sherd claims, fell in love with Kallikretes, and slew him when he made his loyalty to Amenertas plain. Amenertas fled the country with their unborn child and, on the boy's birth, entrusted him with the sherd, which has since passed through sixty-five generations.

The heirloom comes with an entreaty to seek out the queen and destroy her in revenge for Kallikretes' murder. According to accompanying documents, various of Vincy's forefathers have made the attempt and failed. Now, despite his guardian's misgivings, Leo determines to embark on the quest, persuading Holly and Job to go with him. After sundry misadventures they set foot on the east coast of Africa a few miles to the north of Delagoa Bay, near Lorenzo Marques in the then Portuguese territory of Mozambique.

The civilization which they meet there has consistently been misrepresented by the commentators. It is both hybrid and incredibly ancient. Like the Kukuanas, the Amahaggar are a pugilistic people who have grown up amid the ruins of an ancient culture, in this case called Kor. The original inhabitants of Kor were accomplished architects, brilliant engineers, possessing several occult arts which have since disappeared – including the gift of prolonging life. They embalmed their dead, bestowing the bodies in a honeycomb of catacombs within the fastness of their city. They worshipped truth, setting up a majestic temple to her a few miles outside their capital city, which impresses the visitors with its austerity and calm. Apart from their buildings and folklore, little of them remains.

The Amahaggar, by contrast, are a cannibalistic tribe, whose system of inheritance runs along matrilinear lines. This facet of their social organization intrigues the ethnologist in Holly, who explains 'Descent is traced only through the line of the mother, and while individuals are as proud of a long and superior female ancestry as we are of our families in Europe, they never pay attention to, or even acknowledge, any man as their father, even when their male parentage is perfectly well known' (*S*. 82). As with other matrilinear societies, this indifference to paternity liberates women sexually. Much to Job's dismay, it is they who make the advances, walking forward and publicly kissing the male to whom they feel attracted, a habit which Holly (whom they naturally ignore) learnedly compares to the 'early Christian ceremony' of the 'kiss of peace'. A pretty Amahaggar called Ustane thus expresses her partiality for Leo, who duly accepts her as his mate. Tolerantly, Holly comments:

> as all civilised nations appear to accept it as an axiom that ceremony is the touchstone of morality, there is, even according to our own canons, nothing immoral about this Amahaggar custom, seeing that the interchange of the embrace answers to our ceremony of marriage, which, as we know, justifies most things. (*S*. 82)

The matriliny of the Amahaggar, which represents an extension of the marriage customs of Zu-Vendis, clearly draws on Haggard's fascination with alternative models of mating, such as had been recognized at least since the publication in 1861 of Jacob Bachofen's *Das Mutterrecht*.[5] The Victorians found descent through the mother, the emancipating effect of which on sexual behaviour they fully recognized, exciting as well as alarming. Following Bachofen, anthropologists such as Lang and Tylor had convinced themselves that matrilinear kinship, once reported by Herodotus among the ancient Lycians, represented a stage of social evolution through which all societies, including those of Europe, had passed before the imposition of patriarchy. In this respect the Amahaggar, whose name, as various critics have pointed out, incorporates Haggard's own, are a throwback. Holly, who is not in the slightest disconcerted by this custom, contents himself with commenting on its advantages.

The sexual forwardness of the Amahaggar is epitomized by their ruler, Ayesha or She-Who-Must-Be-Obeyed. True to the claims of the shard, she turns out to be Arabic-speaking, immortal, and still keeping watch and ward over the pickled remains of Kallikretes. Ayesha is Haggard's most extraordinary creation, an intellectual and vegetarian, whose forthrightness of mind and manner quite unman Holly and his party. Forgetting their design on her life, they succumb one by one to her power, and to the mesmeric effect of her eyes, which appear at once matchlessly lovely, and immensely old. While Leo, whom she instantly recognizes as Kallikretes reborn, capitulates to her charms, reluctantly deserting the heartbroken Ustane, Holly investigates her well-stocked mind. Its contents, admittedly, possess a late-nineteenth-century ring, redolent as they are of a sort of heightened Theosophy. Indeed, for much of the time, Ayesha conducts herself like Madame Blavatksy as she might have been acted by Sarah Bernhardt. Ignoring her tantrums, Holly is fixated by this baffled, histrionic, amateur philosopher. The reason for his absorption is plain: Ayesha's memory retains impressions of all the ages through which she has passed. She has, however, been out of touch with the mainstream of world culture for some time, and has never heard of the Christians. Her Greek, into the bargain, is more than a little rusty.

Ayesha escorts them to a cleft in the mountains, where flickers the flame of everlasting life. She steps into it, inviting them to follow. But at the crucial moment the process fails: instead of revitalizing the queen, it strips her of all her stored-up resilience, consigning her to her literal age. To the horror of the visitors she shrivels in front of them into a shrieking monkey-like creature, and then into a dried-up relic. Holly and Leo rescue a lock of her hair, and flee across the mountains. After Holly has written up his memoir, they depart again for Tibet, hoping against all likelihood to meet Ayesha once more.

The dominating thematic concerns of *She* are clearly less with gender, politics, or colonialism than with reincarnation. At one point Ayesha and Holly enjoy a one-to-one tutorial on this subject, their thoughts on which follow in the footsteps of the theosophists. Theosophy, after all, was immensely fashionable in 1887, representing as it did an attempt to reconcile science with religion and the occult. Darwin's theories about human development were projected onto a celestial plane, where progress could comfortably be interpreted in spiritual terms. If human beings represented a refinement on the brute, so the occultists increasingly argued, might not such perfectability be perpetuated after death, transporting the soul to higher and higher states of self-realization? Ayesha is the apotheosis of this wish, representing an intensification and prolongation of human energy: emotional, mental, and sexual.

It is possible, I think, to detect three versions of this paradigm in *She*. The first is Holly's fairly orthodox Christian belief, corresponding to Haggard's private convictions, that after death the human soul proceeds to ever greater states of awareness, until it approximates to what Tennyson once called 'the Christ that is to be'. This steers pretty close to an Anglican Broad Church doctrine of felicity to be found, well before Darwin, in the writings of Arthur Henry Hallam. The second is Ayesha's more earthbound view that the individual human perpetuates itself in the flesh, thrusting through the generations to re-emerge in ever more vigorous forms. Her own self-perpetuation is clearly a manifestation of this process, as is Kallikretes' reappearance, after three thousand years, in the person of Leo. There is no particular reason why this idiosyncratic possibility should have emerged, either from Christianity or from Darwin: it does, however, chime in with Hindu and Buddhist beliefs incorporated in the syncretist approach of Theosophy. Interestingly, such thoughts also seem compatible with modern theories of the genetic code, such as have received a widespread airing through Richard Dawkins's *The Selfish Gene*. The transmission of pieces of biological information by means of DNA is as near as modern thinking gets to a belief in immortality. Ayesha's conviction that the personality recreates itself in successive reincarnations could be seen as a rough-and-ready anticipation of this view.

The third version of immortality offered is, I think, the most suggestive. We might call it 'cultural reincarnation'. According to this view, civilizations do not perish: instead they fragment, scattering their achievements through history in encoded shards of survival. The deceased civilization of Kor, for example, evidently once incorporated certain features of ancient Egyptian life: embalming, colossal architecture, hieroglyphic writing. The Amahaggar adhere to an archaic form of inheritance. They also demonstrate aspects of the civilization of the Arabs, a debased and 'bastard' version of whose language they speak, as well as resembling coastal African peoples like the Biswahili. In the scene when they burn embalmed corpses to provide torches for the feast, their behaviour has all of the macabre insouciance of

Nero burning the Christians. The inscription on Vincy's shard is itself an icon of textual recycling, lovingly recreated for us (with the help of Haggard's former headmaster, Dr Hubert Holden) in two forms of Greek, as well as in Latin, and then in medieval and modern English. But the most triumphantly conclusive embodiment of such cultural revivalism is Ayesha herself: Egyptian in her Pharaoh-like ascendancy; Arabic-speaking; conversant with several ancient tongues, as well as with Jewish history, cabbalic lore, and alchemic processes. It is unfair, I think, to portray She-Who-Must-Be-Obeyed, as Elaine Showalter has done, as a projection of sado-masochistic male fantasy.[6] She is much more like an all-inclusive projection of the anthropological or archaeological fancy – a storehouse of all that human civilization has created and endured. Her invincible fascination, inseparable from her historicity, is a product of this. The fact that she, a female, is the object of the quest has far less to do with gender politics than with the slow recognition, by Haggard's late-Victorian mind, that it is the female of the species who perpetuates culture, much as society's recorded achievements may carry the indelible, and selective, mark of the male.

Each of these three types of incarnation seems capable of switching capriciously into reverse. On the biological plane, Holly clearly represents two paths of evolution, one forwards and one backwards, which have unaccountable and tragically crossed, trapping the mind of a Benjamin Jowett in the body of an ape. The glitch which causes the sacred fire to destroy rather than rejuvenate Ayesha frustrates the *élan vitale* by an equivalent feat of retrogression. Yet, as her body shrinks, who or what represents the authentic Ayesha: the splendiferous vision of She-Who-Must-Be-Obeyed, or the hideous fossil that lies at Holly's and Leo Vincy's feet? The teleology of evolutionary processes is an issue that Haggard tellingly leaves in abeyance. To take but one example, sex in *She* appears to be a highly inefficient force: corrosive; lethal; of no real benefit to the species. The ambiguity of Haggard's presentation owes something to the fact that, in spite of Ayesha's optimism, what really intrigues him seems to be less the promise of the future than the lure of the past. Ayesha appears to represent a master race that has transcended space and time; if so, it is a race arrested by nostalgia, longing, and pain. It is when she is most anguished, that she is most unforgettable, and most truly herself.

The pre-eminence of *She* among Haggard's later romances is the result of this superimposition of layers, and their perverse dynamism. For years afterwards, for the rest of his writing career in fact, Haggard made vain attempts to recapture this effect. The book in which he most nearly succeeded was *Cleopatra* (1889), much admired by Kipling, who met its author for the first time that very year. The historical character of the Egyptian queen in this story has something of the sinister, alluring complexity of Ayesha; however, she lacks an additional element which renders Ayesha irresistible: a kind of naïve, girlish romanticism at odds with her scheming. Haggard's painstaking sequels to *She* itself – *Ayesha: The Return of She* (1905) and *She and Allan* (1921) – were, as he himself acknowledged, far less powerful. All of these books are defective in the same respect, in that the worlds they evoke endorse the values espoused by Haggard and his readers. As a consequence they are predictable, whereas the subversive *She* refuses to lie still. When, at the end of his life, Haggard looked back on *She*'s composition, he could scarcely believe that he had written it so quickly. The reason is palpable. His masterpiece, it shares with the Quatermain stories a disturbing yet exciting polyvalence. Like all of Haggard's best writing, it flows like lava from subterranean depths which the imperialist in him could not, and perhaps would not, control.

5

Rudyard Kipling and the Wolves

Four days after the close of the First World War, Haggard spent the afternoon in the study of Bateman's, Rudyard Kipling's house in Sussex, idly reminiscing with his old friend. Facing them, along one of the many bookshelves, ran a complete set of Stevenson's romances; to either side of the long writing desk, rested two cartographer's globes. Haggard was less intrigued by these familiar objects than he was by Kipling's mannerisms. 'In one way he is a very curious man,' he noted in his diary later.

> When he talks, he always likes to be doing something with his hands. 'I must occupy my hands,' he said, and went to fetch a holly-wood stick he had been drying, and peeled and sandpapered it, continually asking my advice as to the process and subsequent treatment of the stick, which I told him to hang up a chimney like a ham. Last time we talked in this fashion he employed himself with a fishing rod and line. (*RKRH* 106–7)

With his fingers thus occupied, Kipling engaged Haggard in a hesitant *tête-a-tête* on the subject of their public reputations. He complained of isolation. 'He is a very shy bird,' Haggard observed,

> and as he remarked had no friends, except I trust myself, for whom he has always entertained affection, and with no acquaintance with literary people. 'But then,' he added. 'I do not think that I am really "literary", nor are you either.' I remarked that our literary sides were bye-products. 'Yes', he repeated, 'Bye-products'. (*RKRH* 107)

The conversation thus noted down took place on Friday, 15 November 1918, by which time both Kipling and Haggard had a considerable body of work behind them, including nearly everything that could be classified as romances. True, the literary tide was turning against them. Even so, Kipling's complaint – or was it a boast? – seems odd. His view of himself, and by implication of Haggard, implies the existence of an establishment, recognizably 'literary' in atmosphere, from which they were by now excluded, a state of affairs which Kipling seems to contemplate with a mixture of resentment and satisfaction.

It is not hard, even now, to identify the leading members of that establishment in the immediate post-war years: men such as John Galsworthy and Arnold Bennet, practitioners of the social novel. Doubtless, these writers now seemed to Kipling to be dominating the scene, perhaps edging him aside. His rueful self-analysis, however, implies that the rift ran deeper than that. Fundamentally, it had to do with the sort of fiction that Haggard and he enjoyed writing, and for which they felt they were qualified, by gift and inclination. To discover what this form was, and in what manner it differed from other more acceptable genres, we must go back to the beginning of Kipling's career.

In 1889, when Kipling had arrived in London after his second period in India, he had settled in lodgings opposite Gatti's Music Hall in Villiers Street, a narrow thoroughfare running between the Strand and the Thames Embankment. In the evenings, and at lunchtime on Saturday, he strolled westwards to Piccadilly, to the Savile Club, where he knew that he would find congenial company, which soon included Haggard. In *Something of Myself*, his autobiography, he recalls Walter Besant's warnings about the cliquishness of the club: soon, Besant predicted, 'things would get like a girl's school where they stick out their tongues at each other as they pass' (*SOM* 84). The only solution to the problem of cliques was to join one. To his father Lockwood in Lahore, Rudyard wrote 'London is a vile place, Besant, Haggard and Lang and Co are pressing me with the wisdom of some set'.

In many ways the morbidly shy Rudyard preferred talking to women, which in the rapidly segregating London of the late 1880s seemed to him to be increasingly difficult. One afternoon, at a tea party, he was introduced to the West African explorer Mary Kingsley, 'the bravest woman of all my knowledge', and walked with her back to his lodgings, talking about 'cannibals and the like'. 'At last, the world forgetting, I said, "Come up to my rooms and we'll talk it out then." She agreed, as a man would, then suddenly remembering, said "Oh, I forgot I was a woman. 'Fraid mustn't." So I realised that my world was to explore again.' (*SOM* 77–8).

To the 23-year-old Kipling, the clubland of the metropolis was thus an alien 'world' that he needed to 'explore'. After six years in India, it seemed as dauntingly inexplicable to him as it did to eccentric middle-aged Kingsley. Tall, hearty, and assertive, she fitted into English society no more easily than Kipling initially did. As a young woman, her bizarre and extrovert behaviour had dismayed the sober citizens of Cambridge – she would, apparently, cavort across Parker's Pieces loudly singing. She had found comfort, company, and relaxation in Freetown and Calabar, and had even hitched her skirts across mosquito-infested swamps in Gabon (or so she claimed). Separated by gender, she and Kipling had this much in common: that their social world was a set of Chinese boxes. Outsiders by inclination, they were insiders by race, gazing at the uninhibited world beyond Europe to which they felt they belonged from the prim respectability of a city to which custom and opportunity condemned them.

At the time, Kipling was evidently finding the experience of returning to England disquieting. Like Haggard before him, his solution was to interpret London anthropologically, probing beneath the urban mask for the aboriginal essence beneath. To Haggard he wrote:

> By the way, I don't believe anything ever was 'primitive' in the world after the time of the Taung's skull. I bet your early Gippos were as stale and as world-weary as any one on the planet now. And I bet, too, they knew it. You've gone back pretty far into history of all ages, and behind 'em, but I notice your people are much like our folk. It stands to reason old man that the world's *very* limited modicum of thinking was done millions of years ago, and that what we mistake for thought nowadays is the reaction of our own damned machines on our own damned minds. Get an odd volume of Tyler's [*sic*] *Primitive Culture*, and see how far this squares with fact. (*RKRH* 139)

The deep-seated kinship between British and 'other' cultures was one which had already interested Kipling for some time. Like many of his educated contemporaries, he saw Indian culture in the light of this relationship. He was, for example, well aware of the view taken by most philologists that the ancient languages of India had evolved out of the same Ur language, or primordial tongue, as the rest of the Indo-European group, including English. He was probably also conscious of the theory held by contemporary jurists, such as Sir Henry Maine, that all European legal systems, including English law, were derived from ancient Indian codes like the *Law of Manu*.[1] In his earliest stories, including those in *Plain Tales from the Hills,* he had projected a double image of India. On the one hand, he habitually trotted out the standard view that the English and the Indians were incompatible races, who mixed at their peril. On the other hand, he tended to stress the buried strata that ran across from one people to the other.

The most impressive exploration of this unity-in-difference to date had been his novelette *The Man Who Would Be King,* first published along with three ghost stories in A. H. Wheeler and Company's Indian Railway Library in 1888. In *Sexual Anarchy,* Elaine Showalter treats this tale as a parable of imperial domination, and an expression of Kipling's ambition to conquer literary London.[2] While recognizing the pertinence of these readings, I think that the story is a lot more revealing if seen in the light of Kiplings's anxieties about cultural similarity and difference, voiced in that letter to Haggard.

Like Haggard, Kipling was well aware of the appeal of the unknown. But, again like his friend, he also knew that the real thrill of adventure story stemmed from the *frisson* of recognizing an image of oneself in unfamiliar surroundings. In *The Man Who Would Be King,* he had decided to appeal to the curiosity of his fellow Anglo-Indians by setting the action just beyond the confines of certain knowledge. In the 1880s, Afghanistan was a territory towards which both British and the Russians had long cast inquisitive eyes. For decades, an assurance of neutrality on the part of the Afghan rulers in Kabul had been an object of British policy. While Kipling was working in India, the Amir had been invited to meet the Viceroy Lord Dufferin at a durbar at Rawlpindi, an event on which Kipling had himself reported for the *Civil and Military Gazette,* later describing the Amir's 'high, big black hat of astrakhan wool and a great diamond star in the centre' (*JB* 139).

British familiarity, however, came to an abrupt halt at the

Hindu Kush, a watershed between the Oxus and Indus rivers to the north of Kabul. The local population of this area, known as the kafirs, were reputed to worship idols, drink wine, and speak a unique language belonging to the Perso-Indian branch of the Aryan family. The Afghan Muslims distrusted them deeply. In Arabic the word 'kafir' means an infidel; the vituperative use of the word (for instance, as applied by South African settlers to the Bantu) was a late application, of which Kipling would have been well aware. By setting the action of his story in Kafiristan, Kipling could draw on his readers' fears and fantasies about a people whom neither the West, nor Islam, had been able to subdue.

The kafirs were fascinating for one other reason. Pale in complexion, many had fair hair, and some were reputed to have blue eyes. Their appearance compared to their swarthy southern neighbours had given rise to a theory that they were descendants of Macedonian soldiers, miscegenated by Alexander the Great's army on its way to India. Certainly, their womenfolk appealed strongly to European tastes. The eminent Assyriologist Sir Henry Rawlinson, who had served as resident in Kabul during the Afghan troubles of 1841–2, once startled a meeting of the Royal Geographical Society in London by the admission that 'the most beautiful oriental woman I ever met was a Kafir. Besides her other charms, she had a great mass of golden hair which, let loose and shaken, covered her completely from head to foot, like a veil.'[3]

Only one European was known to have visited Kafiristan in modern times. In April 1883, William Walter McNair of the India Survey Department, third grade, had taken furlough from his duties in Quetta. Disguised as a Hakim, Tabib, or native doctor, 'with head shaved, a weak solution of caustic and walnut juice applied to hands and face, and wearing the dress peculiar to the Meahs or Kaka Khels', he had slipped across the Afghan border.[4] He had been accompanied by two Pathan guides, and for the purposes of topographical calculation had carried a plane table, done up like a book of Urdu remedies. Arriving at Shahzadgai in the Dir valley, he had successfully cured the chief, Rahmatullak Khan, of the common cold, as a result of which feat he had been hailed as a medical prodigy. For payment he had been given a recently unearthed antique seal, later identified by Rawlinson in London as Babylonian. Proceeding to Chitral in the heart of Kafiristan, he had presented himself to the warlord Aman ul Mulk, together with 'a Waziri horse, two revolvers, a pair of binoculars, several pieces of chintz and linen, twenty pounds of tea, sugar, salt, and several pairs of shoes of Peshawar manufacture'.[5] But his Punjabi accent had soon attracted suspicion. According to his own account of the trip, delivered before the Royal Geographical later that year, 'the Mehter Sahib, or Badshah, alluded to the rumours regarding me, and wound up by saying that as he was a friend to the British, and his country at their disposal, I was at liberty to go about and do as I pleased, provided none of my fellows accompanied me'.[6] Eventually, he had reached Andarthi at the head of the Askari valley, but had been forced to retrace his steps because of persistent gossip that he was a spy. Reporting back to Delhi, he had been reprimanded for this unauthorized expedition by the Viceroy, Lord Ripon, who had promptly taken him aside and congratulated him on his 'pluck'. McNair's deeds were never to be rewarded by promotion in the service, but they were fairly well known among Anglo-Indians. When he died in August 1889, he received obituaries in several English and Indian newspapers, including the *Pioneer* in Allahabad, for which Kipling worked.

The adventurers in *The Man Who Would Be King* however, are taken from a different class from McNair. 'Loafers' or 'Gentlemen at large', they have drifted in from the flotsam of Empire, such as Kipling must often have encountered on his slow trips across India by train, or in the bars and bazaars. Interestingly, in creating these anti-heroes, the diminutive Kipling seems to have gone for his physical opposites. Daniel Dravot is large, shambling, and careless, with a great red beard; Peachey Carnehan is Irishly voluble, beetle-browed, impressionable, and loyal. They make an incongruous pair, both setting off the timid, curious, overworked narrator, a journalist doing much the same sort of editorial job on a local newspaper as Kipling on the *Pioneer*. After he has run a menial errand for Peachey, they turn up in his office and announce their plan: they are going to make themselves joint monarchs of Kafiristan, about which they know even less than he does. None the less, he furnishes them with a copy of Henry George Raverty's *A Grammar of the Pukhto, Pushto, or the Language of the Afghans*, and some old service maps.

They read out to him their hastily compiled contract, which binds them both to avoid alcohol and women, until their ambitions are fulfilled. They set off the following day, promising to report on their progress.

Like McNair, they go in disguise, but as priests rather than doctors. Arriving in the Hindu Kush, they impress the locals, not with medicinal knowledge like McNair, but by their skill at shooting with Martini rifles, weapons unknown to the kafirs, who have only handled matchlocks peddled from Kabul. They achieve some additional prestige by reconciling the tribes of different valleys. Their success is limited, however, until Dravot shakes by the hand a chieftain of the Bashkai clan, whom he calls 'Billy Fish', and receives in return a 'craft grip', the unmistakable greeting between brothers of the Order of Free and Acceptable Masons. Later, when overturning a stone, they accidentally come across a Masonic symbol. At last it occurs to Daniel how conclusively to win over the kafirs.

In order to appreciate the role of Freemasonry in this story, we need to appreciate, less the authentic history of the movement, than what it meant to Daniel's and Peachey's generation, and what it implied for Kipling. The Brotherhood of Freemasons, which had evolved out of the medieval guild system in Europe, did not assume its nineteenth-century form until about 1717. Though the worldwide fellowship had spread outwards from Europe with the growth of the British Empire, in theory its roots were already widely diffused. Remnants of a prehistoric Masonic cult were supposed, for example, to have been discovered, even among the Afghans. The myth of its ancient universal provenance proved attractive because of the *fin-de-siècle* fascination with comparative language and ritual. At the very moment when the philologists were tracing all European languages to a supposed Indo-European homeland, the Freemasons were searching out affinities with ancient oriental cultures that would ground their fast-spreading movement in the concerted march of the mind. In order to support these claims, freemasonry had acquired a fantastic hypothetical history stretching back as far as the ancient Egyptians. Such guesses were responsible for the occult symbolism of the Grand Lodges; the three orders – entered apprentice; fellow of the craft, and master mason – were a bureaucratic contrivance. Though Daniel soon gives himself the air of 'a grand Master of the Craft', he and Peachey never seem to have got beyond the apprentice stage, and Kipling himself would never rise much higher. But Kipling's characters are versed enough at the accepted mythology to regard Freemasonry as a survival from a remote period in human history. In the light of these spurious attitudes, they treat the kafirs as one great, isolated Masonic chapter.

Kipling's description of Kafiristan, and the loafers' reaction to it, is all of a piece with this impression. For Daniel, the kafirs' common roots with Europe account for the whiteness of their skins, as well as the irresistible fairness of their women. 'I won't make a nation,' he cries out euphorically at one point, 'I'll make an Empire! These men aren't Niggers; they're English! Look at their eyes – look at their mouths. Look at the way they stand up. They sit on chairs in their own houses' (*MK* 55). He backs up his theories of racial dispersal with another idea from traditional romance. In the Arthurian cycle, the Holy Grail, the chalice used by Christ at the Last Supper, was supposed to have been brought across from Judaea by Joseph of Arimathea, who, furthermore, was sometimes imagined to have sired the ancestors of the Celts. This speculation has no necessary relationship with the rest of the Arthurian saga, but it represented a Victorian attempt to see the Ancient Britons as emigrants from Palestine, blessed by a generic connection with the Holy Land. According to Dravot, the kafirs are descendants of the same Diaspora. 'They're the Lost Tribes, or something like it,' he cries out,

> and they've grown to be English. I'll take a census in the spring if the priests don't get frightened. There must be two million of 'em in these hills. The villages are full 'o little children. Two million people – two hundred and fifty thousand fighting men – and all English!' (*MK* 67)

Dravot's sudden decision to take a kafir wife has much to do with this perceived affinity. Again, Showalter interprets this as a crude ploy to achieve domination, but the resonances run deeper. Peachey, who mistakes his friend's intention as frivolously amorous, talks irrelevantly about his own disastrous affair with a woman from Bengal. But Dravot is much more interested in establishing an authentic place in the kafir family system. 'Who's talking o' *women*?' he asks Peachey protestingly.

> I said a *wife* – a Queen to breed a King's son for the King. A Queen out of the strongest tribe, that'll make them your blood-brothers, and that'll lie by your side and tell you all the people thinks about you and their own affairs. That's what I want. (*MK* 81)

Dravot's intentions have, I believe, to be interpreted against the kafir marriage customs as portrayed in the story. According to Peachey, recounting their adventures afterwards to the Kiplingesque narrator, one of his and Dravot's first discoveries was that the kafirs practised bride capture. When a squabble breaks out between two adjacent valleys, Dravot sorts it out. 'And Dravot says – "Now what is the trouble between you two villages?" and the people points to a woman, as fair as you or me, that was carried off, and Dravot takes her back to the first village and counts up the dead – eight there was' (*MK* 76).

Now, 'bride capture' was a fashionable theme amongst anthropologists in the 1880s. Evidence for it had been found amongst the Kirghis of Turkestan, in the high mountains 400 miles to the north of Kafiristan: indeed, it had been Eugene Schuyler's descriptions of the Kirghis 'love chase' in a book published in 1876 that had fuelled the ethnographic debate about exogamy. According to the Scottish ethnologist J. F. M'Lennan, the Kirghis custom, a mock battle enacted just before the wedding ceremony, was a relic of seizing a bride in a raid.[7] Even in the mock version, the girl was supposed violently to resist being taken. According to Schuyler,

> the bride, armed with a formidable whip, mounts a fleet horse, and is pursued by all the young men who make any pretensions to her hand. She will be given as a prize to the one who captures her, but she has the right, besides urging on her horse to the upmost, to use her whip, often with no mean force, to keep off those who are unwelcome to her.[8]

Dravot's intended is clearly schooled in a not dissimilar custom. When he makes to kiss her, she bites him. According to Billy Fish, this is because of a (non-existent) Kafir legend that girls are sometimes snatched away by devils, and never seen again. One does not have to exercise much ingenuity to see behind this a folk metaphor for bride capture by an adjacent tribe. The inaccurate anthropological subtext to *The Man Who*

Would Be King would therefore seem to be that the kafirs consist of exogamous clans, and that the girl believes she is about to be abducted by her enemies. In the eyes of the priests, however, the proposed ceremony represents a different sort of exogamous rite: a marriage between a human being and a god. When the girl draws Dravot's blood, she drags the proposed match down to the level of human arrangements, and provokes a revolt. Dravot is beheaded, and Peachey, who has been crucified within an inch of his life, makes his way back to India to tell his harrowing tale.

The Man Who Would Be King, then, is a story about belonging and not-belonging, rather than simply a primer of dominion. In it, Kipling's imagination is exercised with the principal anxieties of his life and work: when is a man an insider, and when an outsider? When is he an 'Aryan', and when a 'kafir'? At what point – in Kafiristan, Lahore, or London – can he legitimately be considered a member of the 'club'? Are all men masons and brothers, or only some of them? When is the 'self' justified in perceiving itself in the 'other', and when is it simply itself? And which of these is woman, in her customary relation to man?

Masonry was a convenient microcosm for all such existential issues. In *Something of Myself*, Kipling tells us a story he picked up as a young child. 'Somehow or other I came across a tale about a lion-hunter in South Africa who fell among lions who were all freemasons, and with them entered into a confederacy against some white baboons, I think that too lay dormant until The Jungle Books began to be born' (*SOM* 8).

Certainly, the Mowgli stories from *The Jungle Books* (1894–5), a set of interlocking mini quest narratives, can be viewed as allegories on the question of belonging and not belonging. Here the lions in the Punjab story have been replaced by a pack of wolves organized along Masonic lines. When Mowgli, a feral child, is discovered wandering in the wild, he is adopted and reared according to principles which would have been familiar to Daniel and Peachey. 'Take him away,' commands Akela, the leader of the pack, 'and train him as befits one of the Free People' (*JB* 9). In effect, this means that the foundling must be induced to respect the Law of the Jungle, a neat oxymoron with overtones both of legality and of unruliness. As explained in the story 'How Fear Came' from the second *Jungle Book* (*JB* 149–67), this aptly named regime instils an uneasy truce between competing individual needs, based on terror of the mightiest. The wolf fears the tiger; the wise tiger fights shy of man: ultimately the fittest flourish, a salutary but brutal lesson which, of course, lies at the paradoxical heart of the very concept of freedom.

The wolves epitomize this paradox. They are free-thinking, high-minded, and fierce. For all their talk of fraternity, they represent a kind of cultural throwback to an age of the crude survival of the strongest. Social Darwinism is embodied in their political system. When Akela's time comes, as he himself ruefully acknowledges, he must defend himself against all comers, like the King of the Wood from J. G. Frazer's *The Golden Bough*, whose first edition appeared a mere four years before *The Jungle Book*. 'Akela said nothing. He was thinking of the time that comes to every leader of the pack when his strength goes from him and he gets feebler and feebler, till at last he is killed by the wolves and a new leader comes up – to be killed in his turn' (*JB* 9). Such fatalism reflects a crisis of identity within Freemasonry, a movement purporting to champion liberty and equality – and which in France had effectively expressed these revolutionary ideals – but which in the British Empire was fast turning into a bastion of privilege and power.

As Mowgli grows in wisdom, the disparity between lupine practice and theory becomes apparent to him. When Akela fails at the fight, he too is driven out. For the first time he realizes that the wolves are heartless, for all their nurturing instincts: in fact, they hate him. At that moment, Mowgli experiences an inrush of that sentiment of attachment which distinguishes him from the denizens of the jungle, and marks him out as human:

> The something began to hurt Mowgli inside him, as he had never been hurt in his life before, and he caught his breath and sobbed, and the tears ran down his face.
>
> 'What is it? What is it?' he said. 'I do not wish to leave the Jungle, and I do not know what this is. Am I dying, Bagheera?'
>
> 'No, Little Brother. That is only tears such as men use,' said Bagheera. 'Now I know thou art a man, and a man's cub no longer. The Jungle is shut indeed to thee henceforward. Let them fall, Mowgli. They are only tears.' (*JB* 19)

Mowgli sets off on the first of his quests, to the village of men.

Yet even here he does not quite belong, and soon runs into conflict with deep-seated human taboos, typically enforced by a priest. When the wolves pay him a visit, they instantly perceive the clannishness of the villagers as an offshoot of their own insensitive *esprit de corps*: "They are not unlike the Pack, these brothers of thine," said Akela, sitting down composedly. "It is in my head that, if bullets means anything, they would cast thee out." "Wolf! Wolf's cub! Go away!" shouted the priest, waving a spring of the sacred *tulsi* plant.' Mowgli's reaction to this exclusiveness is philosophical acceptance of his status as outsider and pariah. 'Again!' he protests. 'Last time it was because I was a man. This time it is because I am wolf.' Like Kipling on his arrival in London clubland in 1889, Mowgli seems to fit it nowhere. He might as well chose the wolves: 'Let us go Akela' (*JB* 62).

Mowgli's next quest is an involuntary one, since he is kidnapped by monkeys. The wolves despise these simians, who are spirited and decadent anarchists, knowing no law whatsoever, not even that of the Jungle. Like the Amahaggar from *She*, they live amid the ruins of a deserted civilization, whose heritage they only partly understand. It is not quite clear *why* the Cold Lairs are deserted; nor why the monkey troupe, whom Kipling calls 'Bandar-log' after the local name for the Bengal monkey, are so feckless. Fundamentally, however, Kipling seems to have projected on the whole scene his own ambiguous, passionate feelings about evolution. The Cold Lairs are clearly the product of a prehistoric monarchic civilization which, like the Kafirs of Kafiristan, worshipped idols. As such, its citizens should have been on a higher evolutionary plane to their monkey usurpers, who none the less act like their etiolated and washed-out descendants. Interestingly, too, Kipling does not reveal whether the monkeys misuse the ruins because they have not yet attained human culture, or because they have forgotten it. In either case, their attitude is one of spineless mimicry:

> They would sit in circles on the hall of the king's council chamber, and scratch for fleas, and pretend to be men; or they would run in and out of the roofless houses and collect pieces of plaster and old bricks in a corner, and forget where they had hidden them, and fight and cry in scuffling crowds... (*JB* 36)

The Victorians were fond of exploring the twin themes of progress and degeneracy. Seldom, however, did they entwine these strands quite so suggestively as in this parable about simian anthropoids, whose behaviour looks forward to the cross-species world of Edgar Rice Burroughs's *Tarzan of the Apes* (1914).

When Mowgli is rescued by his wolf friends, he gratefully returns to the dispensation of the Jungle. By now Akela is dead, and the pack wishes Mowgli to succeed. He refuses, not because he dreads responsibility, but because, as the panther Bagheera sagely reminds him, the wolves have no understanding of the freedom that they enjoy. They are pragmatic liberals, with no schooling in Political Philosophy:

> 'Lead us again, O Akela. Lead us again, O man-cub, for we are sick of lawlessness, and we would be the Free people once more!'
>
> 'Nay,' purred Bagheera, 'that may not be. When ye are full-fed, the madness will come upon you again. Not for nothing are ye called the Free People. Ye fought for freedom, and it is yours. Eat it, O wolves!'
>
> 'Man pack and Wolf pack have cast me out,' said Mowgli, 'Now I will hunt alone in the jungle.' (*JB* 64)

The Mowgli stories depict a paradigm of quasi-human social organization, stripped of the bureaucratic niceties of protocol. They represent this so effectively because they quest backwards: to the domain of childhood, and to the vivid realities of the animal kingdom. When, in 1916, Major-General Baden-Powell formed the Cub Scouts for boys of between 8 and 10½ as an initiatory stage to an already flourishing senior scout movement, he took over Kipling's dramatic personae, lock, stock, and barrel. Every cub pack leader is an Akela, assisted by a Bagheera and a Baloo; implicitly, every cub initiate is Mowgli. And so they remain, even after the Cubs' recent unisex facelift. Kipling, it seems, struck the British social imagination at a pretty responsive spot.

To the extent that Mowgli is a cultural cross-over, he is preparatory to Kipling's next and best exercise in depicting a human hybrid, the eponymous hero of the quest novel written six years later: *Kim* (1901). It is an interesting and amusing fact that the cover of the Centenary Edition of this still popular book features a smiling Indian youth, since, as every one of its readers knows, the story concerns a young Irish boy, orphaned son of Kimball O'Hara, infantryman and freemason, by his wife Annie

Shott. That Kipling's own publishers could employ an illustrator who has portrayed Kim as Asiatic is impressive evidence of how much the novel breaches the Maginot Line between the races. Indeed, the peculiar excellence of *Kim* stems from the deep inwardness of its view of Indian culture. It seems to have poured hot from Kipling's subconscious, spilling out of half-buried memories of an author who had explored the back streets of Bombay as a child, and had spent some of his most rewarding, risk-taking nocturnal hours as a young adult amongst the populace of the Lahore bazaars. *Kim* is a quest for the essence of India, as well as a fantasia on the theme of Empire. That Kipling could combine these achievements bears witness to his talent: it might also cause us to re-examine the whole meaning and thrust of the Raj.

Postcolonial critics have a had a field day with *Kim*, all the more because it obstinately refuses to consign itself to simple minded categories. In *Culture and Imperialism*, Edward Said sensibly refuses to interpret the book as a textbook of empire, construing it all the same as a deep vindication of the colonial enterprise. 'As unique in Rudyard Kipling's life and career as it is in English literature', he declares, *Kim* sensitively registers 'on the one hand, surveillance and control over India; on the other, love for and fascinated attention to its every detail'.[9] These two perspectives are, Said believes, in conspiracy with one another. Kipling saw no disparity between reverence for, and control of, the subcontinent – as we, for example, might well do – because for him Imperialism was a natural and inevitable condition, to which he perceived no alternative. He failed to suppress the conflict between a passion for India's authentic richness and the imperatives of empire, because in his eyes no such conflict pertained.

It is no disservice to Said's reading of *Kim* to probe beneath the political surface of the novel to the deeper confluences the book enacts. For instance, Said notes the versatility and flair with which the Little Friend of All the World sheds and adopts identities:

> He can pass from one dialect, one set of values and beliefs, to the other. Throughout the book, Kim takes on the dialects of numerous Indian communities; he speaks Urdu, English... Eurasian, Hindi, and Bengali; when Mahbub speaks Pashtu, Kim gets that too; when the lama speaks Chinese Tibetan, Kim understands that.[10]

Yet for Said, such flexibility and verve are symptomatic of a controlling will operating pleasurably away from the cultural constraints of England. He also sees them as allied to the political directives of an intelligent (and intelligence-gathering) administration, epitomized by Kim's British mentor, the urbane ethnologist and spymaster Will Creighton, a man who respects the refinements and differences of Indian culture, because he regards toleration as the key to good government, and, through government, of mastery.

Such an account, however, implies that Kim's perspective on India is ultimately identical with Creighton's, a seductive idea which we must resist. The error stems, I think, from regarding Kim as a character in the classical sense, when he is more properly viewed as a projection of the orientalist vision of cross-cultural affinity. Creighton, for example, has no doubts about his Britishness, whilst for Kim, at least at the beginning of the novel, the imperial presence is as remote as it is for his Indian friends. Indeed, for all his delight in diversity, Kim learns of distinctions of power slowly, and with apparent reluctance. Not for nothing does he agree to act as the *chela* or disciple of the Teshoo Lama, the Tibetan Buddhist sage whom he encounters outside the museum in Lahore in the novel's opening chapter, and whose search for the River of Life he intermittently assists, as long as he is able.

Pace Said, it is doubtful whether Kim represents a *policy* as much as a responsiveness, an ideal transmutability. We first meet him squatting 'in defiance of municipal orders' astride Zam-Zammah, the cannon outside the Lahore Museum, an ambiguous act of ownership and of defiance (*K.* 2). When the lama appears, he accompanies him inside the building, and overhears an absorbed Urdu conversation between this holy man and the Curator, a bespectacled and scholarly official based on Kipling's own father, Lockwood. The subject of discussion is the Graeco-Buddhist inheritance, and the complementarity of the Buddhist and Christian Middle Ways. Bearing in mind Kipling's close relationship with the original, who oversaw the planning stages of *Kim*, and who illustrated the result, the Curator's attitudes have to be taken seriously. His conversation is peppered with allusions to the Buddhist scriptures, seemingly culled from *The Sacred Books of the East*, the compilation of mystical literature compiled in Oxford, at the time of Kipling's writing, by the philologist Freidrich Max Muller. When the lama tells him that they are bound upon the same wheel, the Curator agrees. He gives the lama his spare reading glasses, jokily remarking that the present will enable him to acquire merit. Twice the lama recognizes their kinship, the similarity of their respective searches for wisdom: 'we be craftsmen together thou and I' (*K.* 12).

The lama then sets off down the railway to Amritza, and thence by the Great Trunk Road to Benares, protected from chicanery and cheating by the eagle-eyed Kim. This protection has been interpreted as a sign of paternalism; yet it is the Holy Man who provides the direction and sense of purpose without which their ultimate destination would be meaningless. *En route*, admittedly, they must stop over at Umballa, where Kim has a commission from Mahbub Ali, a Pathan horse dealer enrolled as C.25 in the imperial secret service, to deliver to Creighton the pedigree of a white mare, encoded in which are the details of a confederacy of five rajas obliquely controlled by the Russians. But Kim knows little of the purport of the message, and has little sense of its import. Implicated in 'the game', he enjoys it as fun.

On the road they encounter a retired native soldier, who tells them of winning medals for helping put down the 1857 mutiny, only to be reproved by the lama, who informs him that this too is illusion. A dowager from the hills recruits the holy man's help in procuring a second grandson; he agrees out of courtesy, grudgingly abetting this perpetuation of life. Arriving by chance at the encampment of the Mavericks, Kim's father's regiment, they fall in with the Anglican chaplain Bennett and his Catholic counterpart, Father Victor, who recognize the regimental insignia that Kim carries with him as a present from his dying father. When they propose taking the boy into their care, the lama's reaction is one of forlorn terror. 'I do not understand the ways of the white men,' he complains. 'The Priest of the Images in the Wonder House at Lahore was more courteous than this one here. The boy will be taken from me. They will make a Sahib of my disciple? Woe to me! How shall I find my River? Have *they* no disciples? Ask' (*K.* 91–2).

The two Christian priests, set asunder by a denominational divide wider than that which separates any of India's religions, have no answer to this question, which effectively undermines the supposed imperialist purport of the novel. Possessing little conception of genuine discipleship, the army instead provides Kim with education, or rather a utilitarian training. His fees paid for by the beneficent lama, he proceeds to St Xavier's College, Lucknow, where he learns games, maths, literature, and draughtmanship, subjects he absorbs with that zest and detachment characteristic of all his doings. In the holidays he drops in on the Holy Man in Benares, and roams the subcontinent in the resourceful company of Mahbub, to whom he puts the enquiry, nagging but never adequately answered: 'What am I? Mussulman, Hindu, Jain, or Buddhist? That is a hard nut' (*K.* 143).

Mahbub's response to this riddle – that Kim is an infidel and will assuredly be damned – is more convincing than the answer returned by some critics, who see Kim's appointment as a chain man in the secret service as the solution to the problem of his identity. But surely, this unsought-for recruitment engages Kim's flexibility simply because it is the most accommodating of his successive disguises. Witness his stay in the house of Lurghan Sahib in Simla, where he hears incomprehensible voices issuing from a phonograph and then stuffs his robe into it to stifle the words, and plays games with the Hindu houseboy intended to enhance his memory, his alertness, but with few overtones of ownership, or even belonging (*K.*, chs. ix, x). Through all of this, Kim is delectably responsive; yet he is more at home with the lama, or even with Mahbub. When he is deemed sufficiently 'pukker' or ripe in the service, he is sent to the north-west frontier, where he intercepts two Russian agents. Typically, however, the moment of decisiveness which causes him to foil their plans is motivated less by an appreciation of the political threat that they pose than by their clumsy interference with the lama, whose precious paper sketch of the Wheel of Life they rip.

For many commentators, the ultimate burden of the novel is carried by the awakening of Kim to the practical possibilities of adulthood in a scene near the end. 'Things that rode meaningless on the eyeball an instant before slid into proper proportion,' Kipling tells us. 'Roads were meant to be walked on, houses to be lived in, cattle to be driven, fields to be tilled, and men and women to be talked to' (*K.* 282). Frequently, this moment of epiphany is construed as Kim's equivalent to the moment of enlightenment by which the lama escapes from the cycle of rebirth into a promised nirvana. The problem with this interpretation is that it implicitly writes off all of Kim's previous adventures as *maya* or illusion. In so doing, it confuses the overt message of the novel with its effect as literature. Admittedly, Kim finds a niche in the secret service which settles him, presumably for good, and certainly this departure marks the direction in which Kipling's later – and lesser – fiction itself would move: towards justification, mastery, a stress on duty and service. But it is not for this that people read *Kim*, and it was not this mood that inspired it. *Kim* is a great novel because it bucks its own preacherly lesson, pressing the infinite possibilities of otherness in the face of Creighton's logic, Bennett's prejudices, and even Kipling's largely borrowed convictions.

Assuredly, for example, the text is littered with colonial commonplaces concerning the oriental sense of time, the corruptibility of Indian officials, and so forth, all of which Said carefully points out. To see these as essential to the working of the book, however, is to make the same kind of mistake as those who take Haggard's conventionally phrased judgements on African life as the kernel of his work. In *Kim*, it seems to me, these platitudes act like mantras, or piously repeated formulas, floating across the surface of a great mystery, to which they provide a largely ineffective resistance. All of them are mouthed by the narrator, and none of them by Kim. Yet it is for Kim that we read the book, and it is Kim's conscious and subconscious mind that provides its charm and, ultimately I would suggest, its sense.

There is a significant passage about half-way through which describes Kim's arrival in Simla: 'Kim flung himself whole-heartedly upon the next turn of the wheel' we read. 'He would be a Sahib again' (*K.* 148). The imagery connects the boy's temporary immersion in the affairs of the European hill station with the Wheel of Life from which the lama is trying to escape; each, so the implication runs, is an illusion. Kim flings himself with a certain transient zest upon this particular revolution of the wheel, just as he applies himself to the curriculum at St Xavier's during term-time, even winning a prize at Mathematics. Few would deny, however, that he comes most fully to life when the holidays begin, and he takes to the roads. St

Xavier's for him is less a valued training ground than a distraction, delicious because intricate, but of no more worth than a bazaar. Kim's energy is provided not by the syllabus – which gives him about as much sustenance as the United Services College at Westward Ho! in Devon had given his creator – but by a cultural vertigo that drives him. The vertigo, unrelenting even after his culminating vision of normality, is his essence; the exigencies of the secret service, by contrast, are distractions.

Kim's cultural vertigo, I would suggest, was Kipling's too. Always in Kipling's life and work we meet this conjunction: the inner uncertainty, the outer positiveness. 'When he talks,' observed Haggard, watching him playing with a holly-wood stick on that evening in 1918, 'he always likes to be doing something with his hands'. Haggard knew his friend well enough to know that such fidgeting, such pragmatic worrying, were forms of displacement activity. While his fingers were thus engaged, Kipling's mind, as the conversation recorded by Haggard betrays, was engaged with his old anxiety of belonging. This, too, was the subject of his quest romances, and the reason for their popularity. Despite his cherished, outdated prejudices, we still read Kipling to discover who we are.

6

Arthur Conan Doyle and the 'Missing Link'

In 1890, when still working as an obscure medical practitioner in Southsea, Arthur Conan Doyle bought a copy of Kipling's *Plain Tales from the Hills,* which Macmillan had just published in London. He was immediately struck by the freshness of Kipling's way of telling stories. 'I read it with delight,' he admitted later,

> and realised not only that a new force had arisen in literature, but that a new style of story-telling had appeared which was very different from my own adherence to the careful plot artfully developed. This was go-as-you-please take-it-or-leave-it work, which glowed suddenly up into an incandescent phrase or paragraph, which was the more effective for its sudden advent. In form his stories were crude, and yet in effect which, after all, is everything – they were superb. It showed me that methods could not be stereotyped, and that there was a more excellent way beyond my reach. *(MA 252)*

Conan Doyle's chosen method of emulating Kipling's more excellent way was to spin a series of rough-and-ready tales around a single character, an investigator whose quests lead to surprising discoveries. Sherlock Holmes – amateur detective, man of the world, conceited, tobacco-smoking, given to lateral thinking – is a knight errant after the truth, but his exploits do not strictly fall within the sphere of quest romance. In 1912, however, Conan Doyle introduced his less celebrated counterpart, Professor Challenger. In *The Lost World* this splenetic scientist leads an expedition to the Brazilian rain forest to prove his contention that dinosaurs are still living on a remote and inaccessible plateau. He is accompanied by the narrator, Edward

Malone, an ambitious Rugby-playing journalist, by a sceptical colleague called Professor Summerlee, and by Lord John Roxton, a benign and travelled man of the world, who have been entrusted with the job of reporting on the truth of his claims.

Attention has recently been redirected to this story, which has lent its title to a Steven Spielberg film. Historically it is interesting because it marks the point at which quest romance merges with two related forms: detective and science fiction. In part, *The Lost World* seems to have been designed as a reprise of the principal motifs of Victorian quest romance. Its trio of adventurers, vividly contrasted, dependent yet suspicious, are an evident echo of Allan Quatermain and his friends. The plateau which they scale in the heart of the Amazonian rainforest, christening it Maple White Land, possesses a topography reminiscent of Treasure Island. Accordingly, Challenger's colleagues apportion it just as Captain Smollet's seamen had the island, constructing a camp at the near end, from which they mount reconnaissance expeditions, and setting themselves up against their enemies, the apemen, who occupy the far tip, beyond the Central Lake. Like *King Solomon's Mines,* the story features a climactic battle – this time against anthropoids which Lord John Roxton gleefully anticipates by explicitly comparing it with Haggard's contretemps: '"The Last Stand of the Greys" won't be in it,' he exclaims. '"With their rifles grasped in their stiffened hands, 'mid a ring of the dead and dyin," as some fathead sings. Can you hear them now?' (*LW* 139).

Yet of all Conan Doyle's allusions to, and refinements upon, his predecessors, the most suggestive is the character of Challenger himself. In *Memories and Adventures,* his autobiography of 1924, he states that this cantankerous academic was obscurely modelled on the man who taught him Anatomy at Edinburgh University, a 'ruthless vivisector' called Professor Rutherford 'with his Assyrian beard, his prodigious voice, his enormous chest, and his singular manner' (*MA* 24–5). The Challenger of *The Lost World* and its sequels, however, is an evident variation on the theme of Haggard's Ludwig Holly. Like Holly, he is a don, though of Comparative Zoology rather than Classics, and like him he is cursed by an arrestingly monkey-like appearance which causes his associates to think of him as a recessive type. Also like Haggard's simian creation, he is markedly, even morbidly, wary of his fellows. Malone describes him pointedly in the sequel narrative *When the World Screamed*: 'He is a primitive cave-man in a lounge suit. I can see him with a club in one hand and a jagged bit of flint in the other. Some people are born out of their proper century, but he is born out of his millennium. He belongs to the neolithic or thereabouts' (*WWS* 438). Challenger is born out of time.

There, however, his resemblance to Haggard's don ends, for Challenger's misanthropy is written on a far more extrovert scale. Holly avoids women; Challenger has a tiny wife whom he treats like an irritating doll. Acutely shy of publicity, Holly is lured away from his college rooms with reluctance; Challenger mounts expedition after expedition: to discover living dinosaurs; to rescue civilization from an interstellar cloud; to the spirit world; to the earth's core. While Holly hero-worships his young ward, Leo, Challenger has no respect for anything except his own arrogant genius. When thwarted, Holly turns away from his kind in self-hurting mistrust; Challenger, by contrast, erupts.

Challenger's volubility can largely be explained by his circumstances, since it is his misfortune that nobody believes him. This is hardly surprising, since his convictions are often excessive. In *The Lost World*, Malone's friend Tarp Henry, who writes for the journal *Nature*, describes the professor as a 'faddist', adding 'the latest is something about Weissmann and Evolution' (*LW* 13). The observation means nothing to Malone, who has never heard of Weissmann. Yet Challenger's opinions provide vital clues to his personality, to his science, and to Doyle's purpose in writing.

August Weismann, to whose name Conan Doyle adds an 's', was a Professor of Zoology at the University of Freiburg and the author of *Studies in the Theory of Descent* (1882), a treatise principally about butterflies, the English edition of which bore a Preface by his mentor Darwin.[1] So ardent a Darwinian was he that he eventually went beyond his master. Darwin is famous for promulgating the theory of natural selection based on the survival of the fittest, a way of explaining evolutionary facts earlier noted by his own grandfather Erasmus Darwin, and by the French biologist Jean-Baptiste Lamarck.

Lamarck's explanation for evolutionary change had been that that species gradually adapted to their environment, passing on these adaptations to subsequent generations. There is a widespread impression to the effect that Darwin's views were opposed to this idea. In fact this is not the case, since Darwin increasingly insisted that Lamarck's explanation had to be taken into account alongside his own. Even in the Preface to the first edition of *The Origin of Species* in 1859, he had specifically stated that 'Natural Selection has been the main but not the exclusive means of modification'. Darwin was deliberate; he was not dogmatic.

Dogmatism arrived with Weismann. In his notorious essay 'On Heredity', published in 1883, the German biologist rejected Darwin's compromise, claiming that the survival of the fittest explained all evolution.[2] 'Every other theory', he stated, with a dogmatism which seems to invite Challenger's riposte, 'is founded on hypotheses which cannot be proved'. In particular, Weismann rigorously discounted the Lamarckian idea that characteristics acquired by one generation could be inherited by the next. Invoking his famous 'Principle of Parsimony', he insisted that Darwin's concessions to this point of view were unnecessary. Natural selection was all.

In one other respect, Weismann's research extended Darwin's theories. In the late 1870s he had caused larvae of the Mexican amphibian Axolotyl to be slowly exposed to the air in his laboratory. Within a few days, they had exchanged their gills for lungs.[3] Some of his colleagues had explained this metamorphosis as a spontaneous upwards adaptation resulting from an inherent evolutionary force and, as such, contrary to Darwin's hypothesis of natural selection. Weissman insisted that at some remote point in the past his salamander-like creatures had developed lungs but that, because of changes in the lake where they lived, they had subsequently relapsed to fish-like gills. By forcing them out of the water in the laboratory he had, he claimed, obliged them to revert to lungs again. This explanation gave new life to the hypothesis, mooted by Darwin in *The Origin* and subsequently elaborated by Anton Dohrn, that in some life forms degeneration might occur alongside evolution: in other words, that, under certain inauspicious conditions, species could step back in time.

It is the latter theory that seems to have caused the latest obsession in Challenger, who has delivered a controversial paper in Vienna entitled 'The Underlying Fallacy of Weissmannism.'[4] Apparently, Challenger is unhappy at the idea of degeneration, and wants to explain all atavistic forms occurring in nature as survivals, rather than relapses. But he is also convinced, along with orthodox Darwinians, that some characteristics can be explained by adaptation to the environment, without invoking selection at all.

Interestingly, regression is essential to Doyle's story, which depicts several examples of it. Before the expedition even embarks, we meet one instance in the shape of Gladys, the girlfriend of Malone, who participates in the project to impress her. Gladys is a polite and spirited girl who lives in a villa in Streatham, but her appearance suggests degeneration, as does Malone's desire for her: 'that delicately-bronzed skin, almost Oriental in its colouring, that raven hair, the large liquid eyes, the full but exquisite lips – all the stigmata of passion were there'. She stirs a primordial desire in Malone, who is disappointed to find her at ease in his presence, because, 'where the real sex feeling begins, timidity and distrust are its companions, heritage from the old wicked ways when love and violence went often hand in hand'. 'I had learned as much as that,' he adds, 'or had inherited it in that race-memory which we call instinct' (*LW* 4). For Malone, polite society demands sophistication and civility; sexual success, however, depends on our returning to the brute.

But Gladys will not reciprocate Malone's feelings unless he does something heroic. Accordingly, he joins Challenger's expedition to Brazil, where they soon happen upon dramatic instances of survival. Maple White, the dying artist whom Challenger has met on a previous foray, has already shown him a drawing of a stegosaurus, and the Professor has seen a pterodactyl for himself. Challenger and his initially disbelieving friends now observe a colony of iguanodons, an allosaurus, and some great elks. On the far side of the plateau they discover a honeycomb of caverns inhabited by minuscule Indians, who are still at the caveman stage. By far the most surprising discovery, however, is made by Malone when scaling a climber-laden tree:

> A face was gazing into mine – at the distance of only a foot or two. The creature that owned it had been crouching behind the parasite, and had looked round it at the same instant that I did. It was a

> human face – or at least it was far more human than any monkey's I have ever seen. It was long, whitish, and blotched with pimples, the nose flattened, and the lower jaw projecting, with a bristle of coarse whiskers round the chin. The eyes, which were under thick and heavy brows, were bestial and ferocious, and as it opened its mouth to snarl what sounded like a curse at me I observed that it had curved sharp canine teeth. *(LW* 117)

This passage nicely reverses the classical myth of Narcissus: Malone the modern man observes a reflection of himself which takes him aback not by its idealization, but by its revelation of his resemblance to the beast. Later, Roxton informs him what precisely it is that he has seen: 'Missin' Links, and I wished that they had stayed missin' (*LW* 138).

The 'missing link' was a fabled creature that lay between mankind and the apes from which, according to Darwin's *Descent of Man,* man had gradually evolved. Despite decades of research, palaeontologists had failed to locate him. The most likely candidate remained Neanderthal man, first classified by Johann Carl Fuhlrott in 1859. But the idea had long fascinated Conan Doyle, for whom the search for this hypothetical creature corresponded to a scientific detective story. In her essay 'Forging the Missing Link: Interdisciplinary Stories', Gillian Beer remarks on the inevitability of the connection:

> It is no accident that the fascination with the missing link and the rise of the detective novel occur in the same historical period. The phrase 'the missing link' suggests a heuristic search, for a lost link in a chain of reasoning, as much as the search for the evidence of physical remains. It came also rapidly to signify outlandish, even monstrous creatures, as yet undiscovered and, quite properly, *fraudulent*. The search for the missing link therefore frequently shifts from the interpretation of physical vestiges to the detection of human agents.[5]

The hypothesis of the Missing Link, as Beer further remarks, provoked violently opposed feelings in the Victorians, who were intrigued by the possibility of this creature's existence, yet terrified at a prospect of finding him, an eventuality which would clinch man's simian origins once and for all. The most extreme anxieties were provoked by the idea that, in some unexplored part of the world, the link might actually be found alive. As early as *The Hound of the Baskervilles* published in the

Strand Magazine in 1901–2, Conan Doyle had played on these fears, setting his story in a remote part of Dartmoor, in which a degenerate descendant of an aristocratic line works his bestial will through the agency of an equally ferocious dog.

In *The Lost World,* Conan Doyle goes further. Like Dartmoor, but more exotically placed, Maple White Land plays host to the primitive. In it Challenger solves a different mystery from the one he set out to solve. In pursuit of primordial giant lizards, he inadvertently uncovers the Missing Link. But there is a crucial difference from Holmes. For all his apparent respectability, Holmes is quite prepared to admit that he has an affinity with the miscreants it is his job to expose: 'I have always had an idea', he tells Watson in a moment of candour, 'that I would have made a highly efficient criminal'. Challenger, by contrast, insists on the scientist's prerogatives of separation and detachment. Challenger investigates the beast; it is essential for this activity that he should not be one.

The sequel confounds this very assumption. In a nocturnal raid on the camp, the apemen capture Challenger and Summerlee. They then show them off in front of their gibbering companions, at which point Malone and Roxton steal up to observe the proceedings. When they observe Challenger and his captor side by side, they have difficulty distinguishing between the ape king and the Professor, whom Malone describes thus:

> He had lost his hat, and his hair, which had grown long in our wanderings, was flying in wild disorder. A single day seemed to have changed him from the highest product of modern civilisation to the most desperate savage in South America. Beside him stood his master the king of the ape-men. In all things he was, as Lord John had said, the very image of our Professor, save that his colouring was red rather than black. The same short, broad figure, the same heavy shoulders, the same forward hang of the arms, the same bristling beard merging itself in the hairy chest. Only above the eyebrows, where the sloping forehead and low, curved skull of the ape-man were in sharp contrast to the broad brow and magnificent cranium of the European, could one see any marked difference. At every other point the king was an absurd parody of the Professor. (*LW* 144)

So close is Challenger's appearance to that of his brute opponents, that the Indians come to fear him. He even grows sensitive when the monkey monarch is criticized. 'The king of the ape-men was really a creature of great distinction,' he remarks defensively, 'a most remarkably handsome and intelligent personality. Did it not strike you?' (*LW* 148). Tactfully, Malone concurs.

By the time they reach London, Challenger has sufficiently regained his sense of evolutionary superiority to blame the anthropoids for destroying his photographs of the dinosaurs. Yet he provides no evidence of the existence of the anthropoids themselves. The inference is that he has no need publicly to parade the Missing Link, because he manifests the characteristics of this fabled creature in his own defiant person. The result is an odd reversal, as if Holmes had been implicated in a murder. By the end of the story the Professor represents that rare phenomenon: the criminal as detective, or the scientist as exhibit.

No wonder Challenger resists the parallel between himself and the apemen, since it flies right in the face of his theories. Seemingly, the ape has not survived in Challenger so much as reappeared. In effect, he vividly illustrates the validity of Weismann's ideas about degeneration, a theory which he overtly rejects. What has caused Challenger thus to revert? He himself gives the clue. He has, he asserts, been obliged to adopt his bellicose stance because London is populated by primitives. When harangued at the public meeting, he protests: 'I have mentioned the ape-men, and I cannot forbear from saying that some of the sounds which now meet my ears bring back most vividly to my recollection my experiences with those interesting creatures' (*LW 182*). Throughout the expedition he and Summerlee joke about the supposed similarity between the primitives whom they encounter and the bourgeois citizens of England, particularly the gentlemen of the press. In Maple White Land, moreover, Challenger's behaviour is quite reasonable; only when he returns to a barrage of hostile criticism does his notorious irascibility recur, thus suggesting that a whole subspecies, *homo anglicanus*, has reverted to the brute. In defence of his outrageous finds, he is forced to adapt to this environment, endorsing in so doing a salient principle of Lamarckian biology. In this respect alone does his behaviour, along with his writings, contradict Weismann.

Does Challenger represent evolutionary success or failure? Conan Doyle's answer seems to be that he embodies both.

Certainly he helps to quell the beast, since, before they leave Maple White Land, he and his companions exterminate most of the apemen, reducing the remainder to a condition of menial servitude in which they become 'hewers of wood and drawers of water' (*LW* 162). The implication here is that, in South America at least, the Missing Link is doomed.

Yet we cannot ignore the fact that Challenger's success on this and subsequent expeditions is the result of uncouth energies within himself. To the extent that he manages to suppress the apemen, therefore, Challenger can be seen as having quelled the primordial elements, both beyond and within himself. A reading of the book which suggested mere evolutionary triumph, however, would do scant justice to Conan Doyle's insight. Challenger's achievement is the result of precisely that restless, anarchic energy displayed by his subhuman foes.

In effect, Challenger is a compound of different kinds of survival. His boorishness, his determination to succeed, his impatience with opposition and the hierarchical niceties of his profession, all seem to be residues of the earliest stage of societal development, the world of hunter-gatherers. His scientific skill and organizational ability, by contrast, manifest the same instincts refined through centuries of what the Victorians liked to call 'civilization' – in other words, literate town-dwelling. Challenger is an allegorical cross-section of the development of man.

7

'You write the history of the world'

In late middle age, with his literary career largely behind him, Haggard was visited by a recurrent dream, which he came to see as a comment on his profession (*DML* 86–8). In it, he would be led by a faceless guide who in a 'pictured silence' showed him an escarpment populated by golden figures 'which I take it are images and not alive'. In a cleft in the cliff he saw a lake surrounded by tall cedars and pines, from which flowed cascades to the plain beneath. At right angles to the cliff face ran a broad river 'that, like the Nile, floods the lands at certain intervals and makes them bear a hundredfold'. On its east bank, beyond a mountain range, the daylight opened like a fan until it stretched right across the water 'as in the funeral painting of Old Egypt the image of the goddess Nout bends across the heavens and holds them in embracing arms'. On the far bank rose a great city with domes and palaces, while between this settlement and river, and slightly below the level of the plain, stood a house in which the author, some years younger than his dreaming self, sat writing at his desk.

The dreaming presence entered this house, and stood in the corner of the room, watching the young Haggard bent over his papers. 'At what do I work?' the dreamer asked his guide. He answered 'You write the history of the world.'

Haggard reacts to this answer with relief, since it implies that his younger embodiment is absorbed in fact rather than fantasy. Yet evidently the dream is a comment on the writing of romances, and the figure at the desk is toiling over his early successes such as *King Solomon's Mines* and *She*. Evidently, too, its iconography draws on Haggard's memories of Egypt, a country which he had visited on several occasions. The Nile itself had long inundated the nineteenth-century imagination. In Haggard's lifetime, Generals Gordon and Kitchener had fought modern battles along its banks; yet the water course still seemed infinitely old and strange. In fact, it was the oldest river known to European man, described as long ago as Herodotus, and yet, until Burton and Speke's expeditions of 1857–8, and Speke and Grant's further exploration of 1862, nobody had known where it rose. As a symbol of ageless enigma, the Nile was irreproachable. In Haggard's dream, its source seems to lie along an unreachable plateau, rather like Professor Challenger's Maple White Land, except that the figures inhabiting it are gilded and idealized. In fact they seem to exist in a sort of pre-urban Eden, predating the organized city that lies down in the plain. The valley is fertile, yet like the Nile valley it owes all of its fecundity to the annual flooding of the river. The writer in the house has his back to the scene, his attention buried in his papers, but it is from impressions of the landscape behind him that he draws. Like the river, he feeds on distant sources which the dreamer, his older self, is relieved to find are real.

The four authors covered in this book were all seekers after origins. Stevenson looked for his in childhood, in the pre-moral world of boys; Haggard sought the roots of Western man in his African counterparts, concluding that little divided them, and constructing successive versions of that fascinating creature, the white man beyond the black. Kipling drew on constructs of Aryan, Indo-European humankind in the face of which the supposed sophistication of modern city dwellers, which at one level so alienated him, was of little account. Conan Doyle quested back further still, to mankind's primordial past – so far indeed that man merged with his ape ancestors – and further still, to the giant saurians of the Jurassic age. Each of these writers went further than his predecessors: Stevenson to boyhood and maritime history; Haggard to a still extant exoticism; Kipling to common cultural boundaries; and Conan Doyle to prehistoric evidences. In sum, however, their expeditions addressed the sources of humanity itself. As elusive as the source of the Nile, this too was the subject of Haggard's dream.

In his autobiography, Haggard is relieved to discover that the young man sitting writing romances had been no fantasist, because the reality of lived experience underlay his life's work. His three fellow writers shared similar feelings about their craft, and the genre it sustained. Though it resembled an act of escape, quest romance was in effect a search for the truth. Not, of course, truth as Gaskell, Eliot, or Disraeli would have recognized it: the social problems of industrial society interested these writers little, and social justice less. They were not concerned about the state of the drains, or even overtly about the nation's moral well-being. In part, they were weary of such matters; yet there was also a bit of them which recognized that, unless the contemporary human creature *homo sapiens*, and more particularly his European variant, discovered his essential nature, all such questions would ultimately prove to be vain. The Golden Fleece of quest romance, allied to the Holy Grail of Anthropology, was the nature of man himself.

Modern critics are in danger of misconstruing this search, because the cultural semantics of the twentieth century have been somewhat different from those of the nineteenth. Nowadays we take our cultural bearings from our current situation. At one level modernism cancelled out history, and postmodernism tends to rehash it. Increasingly, we honour the past as pastiche. But the great late Victorians thought very differently. For them, the question of authentic sources was important because it explained the significance of the present. You and I are capable of separating causality from inscription: we are, we believe, who we chose to be. But for Haggard's contemporaries, as Victorian ethnographic monograph after Victorian ethnographic monograph demonstrates, the question of origin was identical with that of meaning.

Nothing illustrates this mindset more adequately than the ambiguity with which Victorian people used the term 'primitive'. For us, it is rank with racial offence, and we avoid it. But the Victorians did not speak only of primitive peoples; they also spoke of the 'Primitive Church', meaning by that the original Church, the true Church, the body which they ought to try to reconstruct. Successive ecclesiastical movements in the nineteenth century – the Evangelical and Oxford Movements, for example – were attempts to revive this lost dispensation. By the same token, there was a corner of the Victorian mind which believed, sometimes quite explicitly, that 'primitive society' was cognate with society itself, and primitive man was cognate with man. The apologetics of Imperialism, so offensive to us, were always troubled by this suspicion, which ultimately rendered colonial domination invalid. Indeed, it might even be argued that the very energy of suppression that informed certain aspects of the imperial enterprise stemmed from an uneasy recognition of kinship with the other, the colonial subject. Why else does Kipling, that consummate crosser of cultural boundaries, insist so stridently on difference? One answer is that the affinities he had observed between different peoples were uncomfortably close. To a large extent, for Kipling as for his near-contemporaries, what they had been was what they were.

An objection might be lodged that these are not proper 'literary' questions. The effect of such a remark would be to question the meaning of the 'literary', a category of which several of the writers we have been discussing were markedly suspicious. The whole purport of Haggard's dream was that writing justified itself by transcending its own boundaries. Scorning territorialism, the cultural discourse of the late nineteenth century flowed across such definitions into what Gillian Beer has called 'open fields'.[1]

For this reason a natural elision occurred at the *fin de siècle* between quest romance and science fiction. To some degree this development had been anticipated by Jules Verne: to which genre does *Twenty Thousand Leagues Beneath the Sea* (1869) belong? *The Lost World,* and Conan Doyle's other Challenger stories, also fit both descriptions. The true point of transition between these two genres in England, however, is encountered in the work of H. G. Wells. *The First Men in the Moon* (1901) is both a quest romance and a piece of science fiction, one that interestingly anticipates the future while investigating a celestial body immense, craggy, and old. Significantly, in several of Wells's most suggestive stories, his travellers do not seem to know quite in what direction they are travelling. The lone voyager in *The Time Machine* (1895) twists his control bar backwards and then forwards, but wherever his destination lies – at the dawn of creation, or in an exhausted future – he bumps up against the same ultimate questions, the same last things.

The dreaming-up of the time machine took adventure fiction into new realms. We ourselves continue to rework and reshape quest motifs in epics of space and intergalactic travel. This activity fascinates us because we have turned the cultural logistics of the Victorians on their head. For us now, what we are is what we might become. But whether we meet ourselves as Daleks in *Doctor Who,* whether we fight our demon as Darth Vader in *Star Wars* or, as in Fred Hoyle's *The Great Cloud,* encounter intelligence in the shape of a nebula, we can say to the writers of science adventure, as certainly as Haggard was told by his dream guide, 'You write the history of the world.'

Notes

CHAPTER 1. THE QUEST

1. Elaine Showalter, *Sexual Anarchy: Gender and Culture at the fin de siècle* (London: Bloomsbury, 1991).
2. Edward W. Said, *Culture and Imperialism* (London: Chatto & Windus, 1993), 227.

CHAPTER 2. 'THE CATAWAMPUS OF ROMANCE'

1. Andrew Lang, *Myth, Ritual and Religion* (2 vols.; London: Longman, 1887). See especially ii, 308.
2. Charles Kingsley, *The Heroes or Greek Fairy Tales for my Children. With Eight Illustrations by the Author* (Cambridge: Macmillan, 1856), pp. xvi–xvii.
3. Thomas Carlyle, *On Heroes, Hero-Worship and the Heroic in History* (London: James Fraser, 1841).
4. Thomas Hughes, *Tom Brown's Schooldays* (Cambridge: Macmillan, 1857), 184.
5. Hughes, *Tom Brown*, 313.
6. For a shrewd account of these developments, see Laurel Brake, 'Writing, Cultural Production, and the Periodical Press in the Nineteenth Century' in J. B. Bullen (ed.), *Writing and Victorianism* (London: Longman, 1997), 54–72.
7. Elaine Showalter, *Sexual Anarchy: Gender and Culture at the fin de siècle* (London: Bloomsbury, 1991), 76–9.
8. Quoted in ibid., 88.
9. Gillian Beer, *Darwin's Plots: Evolutionary Narrative in Darwin, George Eliot and Nineteenth Century Fiction* (London: Routledge & Kegan Paul, 1983), *passim*.
10. Andrew Lang, 'Realism and Romance', *Contemporary Review*, 52 (Nov. 1887), 684.

11. The most comprehensive account of the rise of Anthropology in the period in question, and its cultural consequences, is George W. Stocking, Jr., *Victorian Anthropology* (New York: Free Press, 1987).
12. The incident occurred in 1917. The practical jokers were two schoolgirls, Elsie Wright and her cousin Frances Griffiths, who drew a troupe of cavorting fairies in sepia on card, pinned them to toadstools in a Yorkshire dell, and took photographs with a box camera. When Doyle was duped into championing their claims, the case came to be known as the affair of the Cottingley Fairies. See Doyle, *The Coming of the Fairies* (London: Hodder & Stoughton, 1921). For a succinct account of the affair, see Jennifer Green-Lewis, *Framing the Victorians: Photography and the Culture of Realism* (Ithaca and London: Cornell University Press, 1996), 230–1.

CHAPTER 3. BEYOND THE LIGHTHOUSE: STEVENSON'S *TREASURE ISLAND*

1. Quoted in George Speaight, *Juvenile Drama: The History of the English Toy Theatre*, with a Foreword by Ralph Richardson (London: Macdonald, 1946), from which the other observations in this paragraph are also taken.
2. Blackbeard, first acted on the adult stage by Mr Helme in 1798, appears to lie behind Captain Flint, the invisible prime mover of *Treasure Island*, though, as the Squire informs the Doctor at one point, 'Blackbeard was a child to Flint' (*TI* 31).
3. For the biographical facts and details of the journeys, see especially Jenni Calder, *R.L.S: A Life Study* (London: Hamish Hamilton, 1980). For the persistent influence of Scotland in Stevenson's work, see also Calders's *Stevenson and Victorian Scotland* (Edinburgh: Edinburgh University Press, 1981) as well as David Daiches, *Robert Louis Stevenson and his World* (London: Thames & Hudson, 1973).
4. Calder, *R.L.S.*, 166–7.

CHAPTER 4. RIDER HAGGARD'S AFRICAN ROMANCES

1. Lilias Rider Haggard, *The Cloak that I Left: A Biography of the Author Henry Rider Haggard K.B.E.* (London: Hodder & Stoughton, 1951), 121–2.
2. Published at Haggard's own expense, this neglected book sheds much light on his attitudes to Africa. For a less sympathetic account of his politics, see Ngugi wa Thiong'o, *Decolonizing the Mind* (London: James Currey, 1986), 12, 18.

3. Edward Burnett Tylor, *Primitive Culture* (London: John Murray, 1871). Tylor is the fittest candidate for the title 'founding father of Anthropology'. He was read by many of the time, including most of the authors mentioned in this study. Setting out his observations thematically, his book draws on a wide spectrum of cultures to investigate the nature of the human mind, particularly in its ritualistic manifestations. For the ambivalence with which the Victorians frequently employed the now taboo term 'primitive', see Chapter 7 below.
4. Joseph Thomson, *Through Masai Land* (London: Sampson Low, 1885). For Haggard's acknowledgement of his debts for information, see the endnote 'Authorities' attached to *Allan Quatermain.* The very existence of such a note at the end of a work of fiction is evidence of the author's anthropological anxieties, for, as its wording itself concedes, 'a novelist is not usually asked, like an historian, for his "Quellen"'.
5. J. J. Bachofen, *Das Mutterrecht* (Stuttgart, 1861). The late Victorians evidently found matriliny both fascinating and threatening. For the mesmeric appeal which the subject held at the time, see my essay 'Anthropology as Consolation: The Strange Case of Motherkin', in Robert Fraser (ed.), *Sir James Frazer and the Literary Imagination: Essays in Affinity and Influence* (London: Macmillan, 1990), 101–20.
6. Elaine Showalter, *Sexual Anarchy: Gender and Culture at the fin de siècle* (London: Bloomsbury, 1991), 78–89.

CHAPTER 5. RUDYARD KIPLING AND THE WOLVES

1. Sir Henry Sumner Maine, *Ancient Law, its Connection with the History of Society, and its Relation to Modern Ideas* (London: John Murray, 1861).
2. Elaine Showalter, *Sexual Anarchy: Gender and Culture at the fin de siècle* (London: Bloomsbury, 1991), 89–95.
3. Quoted in *Proceedings of the Royal Geographical Society,* 10 December 1883.
4. J. E. Howard, *Memoir of William Walter McNair, Late of Connaught House, Mussooree, of the India Survey Department, The First European Explorer of Kafiristan* (London: D. J. Keymer & Co., 1889), 14.
5. Ibid. 24.
6. Ibid. 24.
7. John Ferguson M'Lennan, *Studies in Ancient History* (London: Macmillan, 1886), 15, 181–4. The connection between bride capture and exogamy had earlier been pointed out by M'Lennan in his

Primitive Marriage: An Inquiry into the Origin and Form of Capture in Marriage Ceremonies (Edinburgh: Adam & Charles Black, 1865).

8. E. Schuyler, *Turkestan* (London, 1876), 42. Quoted by J. G. Frazer in *The Golden Bough* (3rd edn., London: Macmillan, 1906–15), ii. 301.
9. Edward W. Said, *Culture and Imperialism* (London: Chatto & Windus, 1993), 195.
10. Ibid., 191–2.

CHAPTER 6. ARTHUR CONAN DOYLE AND 'THE MISSING LINK'

1. August Weismann, *Studies in the Theory of Descent*, trans. Raphael Meldola (London: Sampson Law, Marston, Searle and Rivington, 1882).
2. August Weismann, *Essays upon Heredity and Kindred Biological Problems*, trans. Edward B. Poulton *et al.* (Oxford: Clarendon Press, 1891–2). For the rigidity introduced into Darwin's system by Weismann and other neo-Darwinians, see James R. Moore, *The Post-Darwinian Controversies* (Cambridge: Cambridge University Press, 1979).
3. Weismann, *Studies in the Theory of Descent*, pt. III, 'On the Final Causes of Transformation', Ch. III, 'The Transformation of the Mexican Axolotl into Amblystoma', 555 ff.
4. This title is probably based on *An Examination of Weismannism* (London: Longmans, 1893), by Darwin's protégé George Romanes. Doyle seems to have followed these debates with keen interest.
5. Gillian Beer, *Forging the Missing Link: Interdisciplinary Stories*; Inaugural Lecture delivered before the University of Cambridge, 18 Nov. 1991 (Cambridge: Cambridge University Press, 1992), 9, repr. in *Open Fields: Science in Cultural Encounter* (Oxford: Oxford University Press, 1996), 118.

CHAPTER 7. 'YOU WRITE THE HISTORY OF THE WORLD'

1. Gillian Beer, *Open Fields: Science in Cultural Encounter* (Oxford: Oxford University Press, 1996).

Select Bibliography

Hundreds of works theoretically qualify for the description 'quest romance'. Adventure stories have always been popular, and never more so than in the period in question. The following confines itself to the major romances by the writers whom I have been discussing. For individual titles I have listed the first edition to appear in book, rather than in serial, form followed by the edition in the Oxford University Press's World's Classics or, where none exists, another convenient edition in print.

ROBERT LOUIS STEVENSON

Works

Early editions divide Stevenson's work into 'Romances' and 'Novels'; in practice, the distinction is difficult to maintain. The works conventionally classified as 'Romances' are as follows:

The New Arabian Nights (London: Chatto & Windus, 1882; London: Shambhala, 1991).

Treasure Island (London: Cassell, 1883; ed. Emma Letley, World's Classics, Oxford: Oxford University Press, 1985).

More New Arabian Nights, including 'The Dynamiter' (London: Longmans, 1885).

Kidnapped, being the adventures of David Balfour in the Year 1751 (London: Cassell, 1886; ed. Emma Letley, World's Classics, Oxford: Oxford University Press, 1983).

The Strange Case of Dr Jekyll and Mr Hyde (London: Longmans, 1886; ed. Emma Letley, World's Classics, Oxford: Oxford University Press, 1987).

The Black Arrow (London: Cassell, 1888; Penguin Popular Classics, 1995).

The Master of Ballantrae (London: Cassell, 1889; ed. Emma Letley, World's Classics, Oxford: Oxford University Press, 1983).

Island Nights' Entertainments (London: Cassell, 1893).
Catriona: A sequel to 'Kidnapped', being the memoirs of the further adventures of David Balfour at home and abroad (London: Cassell, 1893; ed. Emma Letley, World's Classics, Oxford: Oxford University Press, 1986).
The Weir of Hermiston: An Unfinished Romance [posthumous] (ed. Sidney Colvin, London: Chatto and Windus, 1896; ed. Karl Miller, Penguin Classics, Harmondsworth: Penguin, 1996).

With Lloyd Osbourne, Stevenson also wrote:

The Wrong Box (London: Longmans, 1889; Oxford Popular Fiction, Oxford: Oxford University Press, 1995).
The Wrecker (London: Cassell, 1892).
The Ebb-Tide (London: Heinemann, 1894; Everyman, 1995).

Biographies

Balfour, Graham, *The Life of Robert Louis Stevenson* (London: Heinemann, 1901. Intimate, venerable, a trifle hagiographic.
Daiches, David, *Robert Louis Stevenson and his world* (London: Thames & Hudson, 1973). An irreplaceable portrait by a great lover of Edinburgh; hence particularly strong on the cultural and geographical context.
Calder, Jenni, *R.L.S: A Life Study* (London: Hamish Hamilton, 1980). An affectionate and incisive miniature.
McLynn, Frank, *Robert Louis Stevenson: A Biography* (London: Hutchinson, 1993). The latest, frankest, and fullest.

Critical Studies

Keely, Robert, *Robert Louis Stevenson and the Fiction of Adventure* (Cambridge, Mass.: Harvard University Press, 1974). The most complete study of the relationship between Stevenson and the quest genre.
Miller, Karl, *Doubles: Studies in Literary History* (Oxford: Oxford University Press, 1985). An incisive study by a fellow Scot of the theme of doubleness which Stevenson shares with other Caledonian authors. See especially chapter XI, 'Queer Fellows'.
Showalter, Elaine, 'Dr Jekyll's Closet', chapter 6 of *Sexual Anarchy: Gender and Culture at the fin de siècle* (London: Bloomsbury, 1991). A salacious investigation into Stevenson's purported sexual ambivalence. I do not believe a word of it, but you might.
Stevenson, Robert Louis, 'A Gossip on Romance', in *Memories and Portraits, Memories of Himself: Selections from his Notebook* (Tusitala Edition, London: Heinemann, 1924). Gives us Stevenson's own impression of the genre within which he was working.

RIDER HAGGARD

Works

Haggard's fiction was prolific, and not all of the same standard: much of it, moreover, is out of print. In this study I have concentrated on the early African stories, but Haggard also set tales in places as far apart as Tibet and South America. In chronological order, the more significant are:

King Solomon's Mines (London: Cassell, 1885; ed. Dennis Butts, World's Classics, Oxford: Oxford University Press, 1989).

She: A History of Adventure (London: Longmans, 1887; ed. Daniel Karlin, World's Classics, Oxford: Oxford University Press, 1991).

Allan Quatermain, being an account of his further adventures and discoveries in company with Sir Henry Curtis, Bart, Commander John Good R.N. and one Umslopogaas (London: Longmans, 1887; ed. Dennis Butts, World's Classics, Oxford: Oxford University Press, 1995).

Maiwa's Revenge: The War of the Little Hand (London: Longmans, 1881).

Cleopatra: being an account of the fall and vengeance of Hamarchis, the royal Egyptian, as set forth by his own hand (London: Longmans, 1889).

Eric Brighteyes (London: Longmans, 1891; New York: Zebra, 1983).

Nada the Lily (London: Longmans, 1892; San Bernardino, Calif.: Borgo, 1980).

Ayesha – the Return of She (London: Ward, Lock & Co., 1905; Target Books, 1986).

Marie (London: Cassell, 1912).

Child of Storm (London: Cassell, 1913).

Finished (London: Ward, Lock & Co., 1917).

Moon of Israel: A Tale of Exodus (London: John Murray, 1918).

She and Allan (London: Hutchinson, 1921; San Bernardino, Calif.: Borgo, 1980).

With Andrew Lang, Haggard also wrote:

The World's Desire [a novel-sequel to *The Odyssey*] (London: Longmans, 1980).

Biographies

Haggard, H. Rider, *The Days of My Life*, ed. C. J. Longman (London: Longmans, 1926). In this thematically organized autobiography Haggard shows an understandable tendency to withdraw behind a decent façade. Its chapters on religion and politics, however, are revealing enough, as are its thoughts on fiction.

Haggard, Lilias Rider, *The Cloak that I Left: A Biography of the Author Henry Rider Haggard K.B.E.* (London: Hodder & Stoughton, 1951). This life by Haggard's daughter, though predictably over-respectful, tells us much about the private man.

Morton, Cohen, *Rider Haggard: His Life and Works* (London: Hutchinson, 1960). A scholarly portrait by an author who knows the context well.

Ellis, Peter Berresford, *H. Rider Haggard: A Voice from the Infinite* (London: Routledge & Kegan Paul, 1978). Though he is skimpy on Haggard's childhood, and over-impressed by his mysticism, Ellis's chapters on the African years are informative and compelling.

Pocock, Tom, *Rider Haggard and the Lost Empire* (London: Weidenfeld & Nicolson, 1993). A thorough book which situates Haggard in relation to the imperial ideal. It is thus at loggerheads with Chapter Four above, which argues that his work is worthwhile precisely when it transcends any such limitation.

Critical Studies

Greene, Graham, 'Rider Haggard's Secret', in *Collected Essays* (London: The Bodley Head, 1969), 209–14. A provocative view by a fellow writer of adventure.

Haggard, H. Rider, 'Fact and Fiction', *The Athenaeum*, No. 3063 (10 July 1886), 50; No. 3066 (31 July 1886), 144. The artistic manifesto sketched in these pieces is strongly relevant to the argument in Chapter 7 above.

Katz, Wendy, *Rider Haggard and the Fiction of Empire: A Critical Study of British Imperial Fiction* (Cambridge: Cambridge University Press, 1987). Interprets Haggard's work in the light of high imperialism; consequently possesses the same drawbacks as Pocock's biography.

Showalter, Elaine, 'King Romance', chapter five of *Sexual Anarchy: Gender and Culture at the fin de siècle* (London: Bloomsbury, 1991). Contains a fashionable interpretation of *She*, which jumps to a few questionable conclusions.

RUDYARD KIPLING

Works

Kipling's writings raise the question of generic definition to a high degree. Though he thought of himself as an author of romances, not many of his works fit comfortably into the quest genre. A brief list of those works which arguably belong to, or impinge upon, the tradition of quest romance might run:

'The Man Who Would Be King' from *The Phantom Rickshaw and Other Stories* (Allahabad: A. H. Wheeler & Co., 1888; London: Sampson Low & Co., 1890); *The Man Who Would Be King and Other Stories*, ed. Louis Cornell (World's Classics, Oxford: Oxford University Press, 1995).

The Jungle Books (London: Macmillan, 1894 and 1895; ed. W. W. Robson, World's Classics, Oxford: Oxford University Press, 1992).

Captains Courageous: A Study of the Grand Banks (London: Macmillan, 1897; ed. Leonee Ormond, World's Classics, Oxford: Oxford University Press, 1995).

Kim (London: Macmillan, 1901; ed. Alan Sandison, World's Classics, Oxford: Oxford University Press, 1987).

Biographies

Kipling, Rudyard, *Something of Myself: For My Friends Known and Unknown* (London: Macmillan, 1937). Informative, and much raided by the biographers, this autobiography represents none the less a fetching act of personal camouflage.

Wilson, Angus, *The Strange Ride of Rudyard Kipling* (London: Secker & Warburg, 1977). A trenchant study by a biographer who knows what it is to write fiction.

Fido, Martin, *Rudyard Kipling* (London: Hamlyn). An eminently readable biographical essay, amply illustrated and in coffee-table-book format: witty, intelligent, and shrewd.

Critical Studies

Said, Edward W., 'The Pleasures of Imperialism', in *Culture and Imperialism* (London: Chatto & Windus, 1993), 159–195. A balanced treatment which opts in the end for suavely stating the obvious.

Showalter, Elaine, 'King Romance', chapter five of *Sexual Anarchy: Gender and Culture at the fin de siècle* (London: Bloomsbury, 1991). Showalter's discussion of Kipling constitutes a neat exercise in projecting the sexual politics of the late twentieth century onto the late nineteenth.

ARTHUR CONAN DOYLE

Works

Conan Doyle, of course, is best known for his Sherlock Holmes books. His chivalric medieval tales *The White Company* (London: Smith & Elder, 1891), *Rodney Stone* (London: Smith & Elder, 1896), and *Sir Nigel* (London: Smith & Elder, 1906), of which he was inordinately proud, hypothetically belong to our genre; in practice, though, they are historical romances. The only stories which are strictly relevant to this essay are the scientific romances featuring Professor Challenger. These were originally published as single works, but have sometimes been issued under one cover since. They are:

The Lost World: Being an Account of the Recent Amazing Adventures of Professor George E. Challenger, Lord Roxton, Professor Summerlee and Mr. E. D. Malone of 'The Daily Gazette' (London: Hodder & Stoughton, 1912; introd. Ian Duncan, Oxford Popular Fiction, Oxford: Oxford University Press, 1995).

The Poison Belt: being an account of Another Adventure of Professor George E. Challenger, Lord John Roxton, Professor Summerlee, and Mr. E. D. Malone, the discoverers of 'The Lost World' (London: Hodder & Stoughton, 1913); in *The Lost World and Other Stories* (Wordsworth Classics, Ware: Wordsworth Editions, 1995).

The Land of Mist (London: Hutchinson, 1926); in *The Lost World and Other Stories* (Wordsworth Classics, Ware: Wordsworth Editions, 1995).

The Disintegration Machine from *The Maracot Deep, and Other Stories* (London: John Murray, 1929); in *The Lost World and Other Stories* (Wordsworth Classics, Ware: Wordsworth Editions, 1995).

When the World Screamed from *The Maracot Deep, and Other Stories* (London: John Murray, 1929); in *The Lost World and Other Stories* (Wordsworth Classics, Ware: Wordsworth Editions, 1995).

Biographies

Doyle, Arthur Conan, *Memories and Adventures* (London: Hodder & Stoughton, 1924). An autobiography composed less with the oblique genius of Sherlock Holmes than with the dependability of Dr Watson.

Dudley-Edwards, Owen, *The Quest for Sherlock Holmes: A Biographical Study of Sir Arthur Conan Doyle* (Edinburgh: Mainstream, 1983). A subtle study of Doyle's intriguing personality: outwardly conventional, inwardly driven, scientific, and credulous in turns. By far the most intelligent Life.

Booth, Martin, *The Doctor, the Detective and Arthur Conan Doyle: A Biography* (London: Hodder & Stoughton, 1997). A comprehensive recent account.

Critical Studies

Bloom, Clive; Doherty, Brian; Gibb, Jane; and Shand, Keith (eds.), *Nineteenth Century Suspense: From Poe to Conan Doyle* (London; Macmillan 1988). Effectively demonstrates how much Conan Doyle owed to his predecessors. See, especially, Howard Davies's essay '*The Lost World*: Conan Doyle and the Suspense of Evolution', 107–19.

BACKGROUND READING

Beer, Gillian, *The Romance* (London: Methuen, 1970). A scholarly and incisive discussion of the genre, tracing the nineteenth-century revival back to the medieval *fons*.

Brake, Laurel, 'Writing, Cultural Production, and the Periodical Press in the Nineteenth Century', in J. B. Bullen (ed.) *Writing and Victorianism* (London: Longman, 1997). A brisk essay tackling the practicalities underlying the shift to shorter fiction in the late Victorian age.

Cohen, Morton, *Rudyard Kipling to Rider Haggard* (London: Hutchinson, 1965). An impeccably researched, and deeply moving, account of their relationship, revealing, for instance, just how much Kipling, supposedly the greater writer, admired Haggard's copious output.

Fayter, Paul, 'Strange New Worlds of Space and Time: Late Victorian Science and Science Fiction' in Bernard Lightman (ed.), *Victorian Science in Context* (Chicago and London: University of Chicago Press, 1997). A beautifully articulated study of early scientific romance.

Green, Martin, *Dreams of Adventure: Deeds of Empire* (London: Routledge, 1980). Interprets quest romance in the light of the imperial project.

Killim, Douglas, *Africa in English Fiction, 1874–1939* (Ibadan: Ibadan University Press, 1968). Faithfully reads it chosen authors against the changing image of the continent.

Sandison, Alan, *The Wheel of Empire: A Study of the Imperial Idea in some Late Nineteenth and Early Twentieth Century Writers* (London: Macmillan, 1967). Historically authentic survey by a recent editor of *Kim*.

Stocking, George W., Jr., *Victorian Anthropology* (New York: Free Press, 1987). A learned exposition of the impact of the politics of nineteenth-century ethnology on contemporary perceptions of humankind.

Index

WRITERS AND THEIR WORK

"... this series promises to outshine its own obviously high reputation."
Times Higher Education Supplement

"... will build into a fine multi-volume critical encyclopaedia of English literature."
Library Review & Reference Review

"... Excellent, informative, readable, and recommended."
NATE News

"written by outstanding contemporary critics, whose expertise is flavoured by unashamed enthusiasm for their subjects and the series' diverse aspirations."
Times Educational Supplement

"A useful and timely addition to the ranks of the lit crit and reviews genre. Written in an accessible and authoritative style."
Library Association Record

WRITERS AND THEIR WORK

Title	Author
Alfred Tennyson	*Seamus Perry*
Anita Desai	*Elaine Yee Lin Ho*
Anthony Trollope	*Andrew Sanders*
Byron	*Drummond Bone*
C.S. Lewis	*William Gray*
Charles Dickens	*Rod Mengham*
Chinua Achebe	*Nahem Yousaf*
D.H. Lawrence	*Linda Ruth Williams*
E.M. Forster	*Nicholas Royle*
Franz Kafka	*Michael Wood*
George Eliot	*Josephine McDonagh*
George Orwell	*Douglas Kerr*
Gerard Manley Hopkins	*Daniel Brown*
Harold Pinter	*Mark Taylor-Batty*
Henrik Ibsen, 2nd edition	*Sally Ledger*
Henry James—The Later Writing	*Barbara Hardy*
Jane Austen	*Robert Miles*
John Keats	*Kelvin Everest*
Joseph Conrad	*Cedric Watts*
Leo Tolstoy	*John Bayley*
Oscar Wilde	*Alexandra Warwick*
Paul Scott	*Jacqueline Banerjee*
Percy Bysshe Shelley	*Paul Hamilton*
Philip Larkin, 2nd Edition	*Laurence Lerner*
Robert Browning	*John Woolford*
Rudyard Kipling	*Jan Montefiore*
Samuel Beckett	*Sinéad Mooney*

WRITERS AND THEIR WORK

Title	Author
Samuel Taylor Coleridge	*Stephen Bygrave*
Shashi Deshpande	*Amrita Bhalla*
Sir Walter Scott	*Harriet Harvey Wood*
Stephen Crane	*Kevin J. Hayes*
Swinburne	*Catherine Maxwell*
Sylvia Plath, 2nd edition	*Elisabeth Bronfen*
T.S. Eliot	*Colin MacCabe*
Ted Hughes	*Susan Bassnett*
Thomas Hardy, 2nd Edition	*Peter Widdowson*
V.S. Naipaul	*Suman Gupta*
Victorian Quest Romance	*Robert Fraser*
Virginia Woolf, 2nd Edition	*Laura Marcus*
W.B. Yeasts	*Edward Larrissy*
William Blake	*Steve Vine*
William Golding, 2nd Edition	*Kevin McCarron*
William Makepeace Thackeray	*Richard Salmon*
Wole Soyinka	*Mpalive-Hangson Msiska*